The Language of Seabirds

The Language of Seabirds

Will Taylor

SCHOLASTIC PRESS
NEW YORK

Library of Congress Cataloging-in-Publication Data available

ISBN 978-1-338-75373-8

1 2022

Printed in the U.S.A.   23

First edition, July 2022

Book design by Christopher Stengel

*For every kid who's had
to speak in code*

One

They say living through an Oregon winter is the closest most people there ever come to drowning. As autumn dies, a ceiling of gravestone cloud settles over the land, pressing heavier week after dreary week. Sooner or later, everyone under that sky feels the pressure, the creeping sense of being trapped. For Jeremy Ryden, it arrived over breakfast on the first day of winter break, which also happened to be his first day of being twelve.

It was Uncle Becker's birthday card that sparked it, the shiny picture of a lifeguard girl on a tropical beach sliding out of the envelope like a bad joke told too loud. Jeremy's mom looked up from her phone long enough to frown, but his dad whistled and laughed, clapping him on the back. So Jeremy, panicking, pretended to like the picture, forcing a smile and counting down the seconds while pressure built over his heart. As soon as he dared, he extracted his twenty-dollar bill and flipped the card over, relieved to find a sweep of empty sand and waves and electric-blue sky decorating the back.

He stared, for real this time, then caught himself and yanked his gaze away, landing instead on the steady drizzle filling their small kitchen window. And just like that, the weight of the Oregon winter hit home, filling his lungs. He felt his dad's eyes on him and turned back to the picture with its beach and sky and impossible freedom, a question jumping to his lips.

"Why haven't we ever been to the ocean?"

His dad choked on his bacon, and his mom set down her coffee with an offended clack. In a moment of rare agreement, they both insisted he certainly *had* been to the ocean, naming a summer when the three of them had trooped the ninety miles west from Corvallis to the coast.

From what they reported, Jeremy hadn't even reached kindergarten at the time, and he could say truthfully that he didn't remember. His mom retrieved the family photo albums for evidence, but when no one was able to find any pictures, suddenly the exact year was up for debate. Apparently knowing the exact year of things was important in a marriage, and it wasn't long before Jeremy was slipping back to his room, leaving his parents bickering over the remains of his birthday breakfast.

The gray December rain pattered sullenly against his window, doing nothing to cover the sound of his parents' increasingly loud disagreement as Jeremy flopped onto his bed. He had woken that morning tight with nerves, thinking this of all days might be the day to let his parents in on what he had recently realized about himself: that when it came to love and romance, his feelings were aimed at other guys. He had hoped to get the telling over and done with, with his mom on hand in case the news disappointed his dad. But that wasn't going to happen now.

Winter surrounded the house, and the house surrounded his room, and Jeremy curled up alone in the middle of it, turning to his hidden stash of fashion magazines for company. Gratefully, he sank into the unchanging glamour of their glossy pages, holding all his secrets in, wondering when he would ever find the words and the courage to let them out.

Six months later, in the clean sunlight of late June, Jeremy rolled down the passenger window of his dad's car and looked out over the Pacific. It was just the two of them now—one half of the divided family that Jeremy was somehow expected to learn to bridge.

"Remember it, Jer?" his dad asked, breaking fifty miles of silence.

Jeremy, his eyes full of white-capped, rolling blue, shook his head.

His dad made a sound through his nose, the short, dismissive grunt that had become part of his regular vocabulary that spring as the divorce ground its way to completion.

Jeremy leaned against his seat belt strap, listening to the wind whiffle past. He wondered if some part of him actually did remember this, if some recognition left over from childhood was why shivers were tapping along his shoulders, why deep down he almost felt like crying.

The road dropped at the next turn, hiding the heaving ocean and sending them past houses with pin-striped lawns, trailer parks with plastic flowers, and small churches with giant signs. Finally, a painted driftwood log announced they had reached Rosemont.

Jeremy read out the directions Uncle Becker had sent, and five minutes later they were pulling up alongside a red pickup in the gravel driveway of the house that would be their home for the next two weeks.

The house was on the beach—or as close to the beach as a house could get, set back from the sand on a shelf of earth flecked with pine cones from the two wind-bent trees standing over it. It was a small house, painted brown, with a ground floor, a gabled attic, and a covered porch facing the water. Someone had left two white shells on the porch railing. A pair of rocking chairs sat to the right of the door.

Jeremy hadn't smiled yet that day, but he did then. Their closest neighbor was the Pacific Ocean. He would be living on the edge of the world.

The porch door opened, and Becker appeared. He was a skinny, handsome man in his mid-thirties, with the same Irish-pale coloring as Jeremy and his father, as well as the same wavy brown hair.

"Big brother!" Becker hollered, leaping the railing as they got out of the car. "Baby nephew!"

"Hey, Becks," called Jeremy's dad. Jeremy fixed his hair while the brothers hugged and punched each other, then had it messed up again as Becker pounced on him.

"Look at this kid!" Becker pulled Jeremy into a one-armed hug, pressing a fist against his ribs. "Not a baby now! Tall like his uncle, freckles like his mom—guess who's gonna break the heart of every girl in Rosemont? You know life doesn't start until you have a girlfriend!"

Jeremy pinched out a smile, earning a barked laugh and a slap on the stomach. His dad was already on the porch, heading inside with the first of their bags, and Becker's hand rose to squeeze Jeremy's shoulder as he disappeared.

"Okay, but how's the old man doing?" he asked, pitching his voice low. "I know things were officially final a couple weeks ago, but man, *today*. This has really gotta make it real for Mike."

Jeremy fought the urge to duck out from under his uncle's arm and run for the house. It had been three whole years since he'd seen Becker, and he'd forgotten how quickly he could leap from noisy joking to buddy-buddy affection. It all made Jeremy nervous.

"Dad's been kind of quiet," Jeremy managed. "I think he's, um, thinking, or something?"

It was honestly as much as he knew.

"Got it," Becker said. "Guess it can be hard to say what you're really feeling, especially when it's something big like this. Well, I'm gonna do what I can to get his spirits up." His fingers dug into Jeremy's neck. "And you gotta work with me, okay, bud? Your dad needs both of us in his corner right now."

"Jer!"

Jeremy looked up in time to miss catching an airborne house key. It bounced into the sandy dirt.

"You've got the room upstairs," his dad called from the porch. "Get your stuff in."

Becker gave him a conspiratorial wink and let him go. Jeremy, relieved, retrieved the key, grabbed the first of his bags, and headed inside.

The house wasn't too bad. The door off the porch led to a wall-papered dining room with a wooden table and chairs, separated from a small kitchen by a counter set with stools. Past that was a living room with a sofa, an easy chair, a shelf of paperbacks, and a decent-looking TV. Three doors opened onto a compact yellow bathroom, a bedroom—Jeremy's father's now—with a quilted bed taking up most of the space, and, in the far back corner, a set of stairs leading up.

Becker clomped inside as Jeremy began climbing.

"Careful when you get up in the night to pee, Jer!" his dad called from his bedroom. "I can hear you squeaking on every step."

Becker said something with a snorted laugh, and Jeremy took the rest of the stairs two at a time, pushing past a white wooden door into the first new room he'd ever had.

He decided immediately that he liked it. The walls stopped halfway up to angle in with the slope of the roof, making the room feel cozy. There was a twin bed covered in blue sheets near the window, a bedside table with a lamp, and a narrow empty closet standing open.

Jeremy dropped his bags and went straight to the window.

Back home, his bedroom view was nothing but an old, overgrown rhododendron bush. Not that he minded. Every summer when it flowered pink and cream, the bees would come, and he'd spend long hours watching them work. It was incredibly comforting, sitting safe and protected, watching the world through glass.

Somewhere in the construction-paper and long-division years of elementary school, he'd found himself carrying that feeling with him—first to the school bus and classroom, then to the family dinner table—until his invisible pane of glass went everywhere: a secret shield and barrier. He barely remembered it was there anymore. He stayed behind it without thinking.

This new window, with its view out over the porch roof to the sand and sky and the whole entire ocean . . . this was something else entirely, from some other kind of life. And for the next two weeks, it would be his.

He let out a silent breath, telling himself he could relax now. He should be safe here. Safe enough to get through their stay with the secret of his heart still locked up tight. There had never been a chance to share it while the divorce was unfolding, not after his mom had turned out to have some big secrets of her own. Not while his dad was reeling from the collapse of his own expectations for love and romance. Jeremy had seen it all, no matter how much his parents had tried to keep from him, and it had been impossible to imagine dragging them back together to share his own nervous revelation, to make them act like a family again just for his sake.

Now they were divorced, the family split, and what would be the point in telling? How would it help, or make anything better? It was best to keep himself to himself. He might tell them, someday, maybe, if a lot of things changed. But for now, he would lie low and keep his heart quiet and be fine enough with this cozy room, and this house, and the sea.

He gazed out, running his fingers over the dusty window, tracing tiny ripples in the glass. They almost looked like waves.

"Hey, dreamer boy, I see you up there!"

Jeremy blinked awake as Becker leaned on the car horn, sending a patch of seagulls flapping and hopping. A raised beer bottle glinted up at him. "There's work to do!"

Jeremy waved and turned for the stairs, realizing as a bird flashed past the glass that his attic room meant he'd be living up between the earth and sky, just like the house sat between the water and the land.

He almost smiled. Everything about this trip was in between. In between the family before and the family after. In between one school year and the next. In between his last year as a kid and his first year as a teenager.

That thought made him stumble, tripping down the steps. He wasn't sure how he felt about becoming a teenager yet. He wasn't sure at all.

Settling in took well under an hour, but Jeremy's father and uncle had still lined up a row of empty bottles on the porch by the time they were done. Jeremy sat with them, listening from his perch on the railing with his arms around his knees.

"So, Mikey," Becker said expansively, waving a fresh beer from his chair, "the bachelor life tasting like you remember it? You ready for this break?"

Jeremy's dad shook his head. "Too soon, Becks." His chair creaked as he rocked. "And this isn't a *break*. I have recommendations to write, all of next year's grant applications, two course proposals that need reworking—I've got plenty to do."

Becker choked out a laugh. "Okay, Mr. College Professor, do your thing," he said. "But don't let that stuff get in your way. This is *your* time out here. You get to decide how you want to use it."

Jeremy's father tilted his head back to finish his beer, then settled the bottle beside the others with a clink. "I know that."

"Tomorrow I'll show you the town," Becker went on. "There's all the touristy stuff on Main Street, the grocery store, that one donut place . . . and, oh, you know, Sandy's Grill." He nudged his brother with his foot, showing all his teeth.

"What about the beach?" Jeremy asked. His voice sounded high in his ears.

The men looked over.

"What *about* the beach?" His dad pointed with his chin. "It's right there. It goes left and right for the entire state of Oregon. Enjoy."

"Gotta watch out if you go too far left, though," Becker said. "Marbletop Cliffs are a few miles south, and the ocean fills the cove right up to the wall. You get stuck out there when the tide comes in, you better either be a real strong swimmer or else know how to fly."

"Why're they called Marbletop?" asked Jeremy.

Becker shrugged. "Why's anything called anything?"

"That's not what you said about Sandy's," said Jeremy's father. Becker grinned.

The brothers turned back to each other, talking in their clipped, lazy style about plans and houses and summer and women. It looked like Uncle Becker had succeeded in cheering Jeremy's dad up, at least. But it made Jeremy feel strange. You'd think his father's marriage hadn't just ended at all. You'd think this really was a vacation.

He pulled deeper into himself, tuning out their voices to listen to the sea wind and the hiss of the waves, watching the birds and families and dogs scattered across the beach. Plans for how he might fill his own time here drifted through his brain: long walks, beach-combing, sleeping in, reading. Maybe his dad would let him build a few driftwood fires at night. Maybe there would be a store or two worth visiting in town.

He shifted, turning to scratch his back against the house, and suddenly stopped, his fingers clenching tight around his knees.

A boy was running toward him, following the last line of sand just before the rocks and dirt. He was around Jeremy's age, with a flare of dark hair and white skin taking on an early summer tan. He ran with his whole body, his hands and feet moving in perfect unison. His shoulders floated above his waist. His face was open, his head held high, his red shorts and gray shirt whipping around him like flags.

Jeremy kept perfectly still, his eyes following every footfall.

What would it feel like to run like that? To look like that while running?

The boy was going to pass right by their deck, and Jeremy couldn't help it. Against all his care, against all his agonizing self-control, he turned his head to keep watching, breathless, until the running boy passed out of sight and was gone.

Instantly, cold fear crashed in. What was he doing? Had his dad seen him looking? Or Uncle Becker?

But a glance told him the men hadn't seen a thing. They were still talking and rocking. They'd missed the beautiful runner and Jeremy noticing that he was beautiful. They'd missed the turn of Jeremy's head and the wideness of his eyes.

It was okay; he was still safe. And for that one, gleaming moment, the glass between him and the world had disappeared.

Jeremy shook himself. He was being ridiculous. Nothing had changed. Nothing here could really be different.

Could it?

Unprompted, Becker's advice to his father slid across his mind: *This is your time out here. You get to decide how you want to use it.*

If that was true, then . . . what if?

His dad had said he'd be busy, so Jeremy would probably have lots of time alone. Nobody else in Rosemont even knew who he was, and he'd leave it all behind in two weeks anyway.

What if, in the in-between, he had a chance to be himself?

Just the thought made Jeremy's head spin, made him want to curl up inside the familiar nest of shelter and safety. But he could already feel it: the warmth of possibility tugging irresistibly at his skin, sinking into his bones, tangling itself into his summer.

Two

TUESDAY, JUNE 26

Jeremy woke on his first beach house morning to sunlight in the window, birds calling overhead, and the smell of frying bacon coming from downstairs. He twisted to stretch his back after the unfamiliar mattress, staring up at the knots and whorls of the slanted pine board ceiling.

So, this was day one on the coast. Day one of the unknown.

In fourteen more days, he'd be waking up like this and packing his bags. Loading up the car and heading back to Corvallis, back to the house. Where all his mom's stuff would be gone.

That had been the final decision of the divorce: Jeremy's dad would stay in the family home, close to his work at the college, and Jeremy would stay with him at least through the summer. His mom was moving to Beaverton to follow her dream job at Nike, the job she'd applied for and gotten in secret, the once-in-a-lifetime career opportunity that had led to her realizing a whole lot of things in her life needed changing. She'd already found a house in Beaverton, but with her work schedule, the move was going to take weeks. The news that one of Uncle Becker's rentals was free after a cancellation had come in the nick of time, and the grown-ups had stopped bickering long enough to settle on the plan: The boys would go to the beach, and Jeremy's mom would use their absence to move out in peace.

Jeremy had been slightly surprised by his own calmness about his mom moving away. It was strange, for sure, after living with her his whole life, but they still talked or texted most days, and he would be going out to visit once she got herself settled. She had already sent him details about the school he would attend in Beaverton if he decided to live with her, along with a list of local attractions a pre-teen like him might like. She was always thorough about things like that, even if she was distracted most of the time now by her all-consuming fresh start. He actually found himself admiring her bravery. He didn't know if he would have it in him to just go for it, turn his whole life inside out, stand up tall and tell the world exactly what he wanted.

So, after the beach, he would be going back to the same place he'd always lived in, but different, and he'd live there with his dad, at least for a while. He had no clue yet what choice he would make at the end of summer, which house he would want to call home. He was grateful he had plenty of time to decide. Who knew how he might feel after his time here in the in-between? Even playing it safe, a lot could happen in two weeks. Would he be happy to go back to the same old room, the same old school, the same old classmates he'd never quite managed to turn into friends? Or would he want a fresh start?

A buzz from his phone pulled Jeremy back to the present. A text had gotten through! Uncle Becker had warned them reception was patchy right on the coast. It was better in town, apparently, only half a mile inland but enough to make a difference. Jeremy reached out to his bedside table.

> You were supposed to text me when you got there. How's the place? Xoxo

A typical text from his mom. Jeremy could see her flashing out the message one-handed while emailing someone important with the other. He tapped out a reply.

> The place is good. I got the upstairs room. The beach is huge. Uncle Becker's taking us to see the town today.

He hit send, then,

> Reception isn't good from the beach. Sorry!

Send again. The little wheel spun beside both messages. Spun and spun. He set the phone down and opened the bedside drawer for his charger, making something thump in the back. He reached in and found a dog-eared book. The cover, decorated in bright primary colors, said *Seabirds of the Central Oregon Coast.*

Jeremy flipped through the pages. *Horned grebe, cinnamon teal, wandering tattler.* Birds had the weirdest names. Or maybe the coolest, actually? He looked up from the book and squinted out the window.

Five minutes later he was downstairs, padding into the kitchen, where his dad was drinking coffee at the counter. The window was open, and the sun was shining on the water.

"G'morning," Jeremy said on his way to the bread basket. His dad looked up, watching him closely, and Jeremy realized with a jolt he had no idea what these minor daily encounters were going to be like now it was just the two of them. Were they going to talk? About what? And who would decide? His dad had changed since his mom began the divorce—turning moodier and laughing a lot less—and Jeremy honestly couldn't be sure he would stick to safe, comfortable topics now. He remembered his bedside discovery and cleared his throat, deciding to get ahead of things.

"Hey, did you know those are Heermann's gulls up on the roof?" he said. "I found this old book, and it says—"

"What are you doing?" his dad interrupted.

Jeremy stopped, the bread bag twisting in his hand. "Um, making toast?"

"I mean, what are you doing walking in here like that?"

Jeremy opened his mouth, then shut it again.

"When you get up in the morning, you wash your face and hands before joining the common areas. You know that."

Jeremy blinked, wondering when in his entire life he was supposed to have learned that policy.

"That's . . . not a rule we ever had before," he said.

His father set down his mug. There were bags under his eyes. Uncle Becker had stayed late the night before; Jeremy had heard the men still talking as he drifted off to sleep, along with the occasional clink of bottles.

"Well, it's a rule in this house. It's basic politeness not to show up with eye crud and pillow lines and hands that have been who knows where. Now go get washed, please."

Jeremy's face felt hot. The unfairness of it—being called out for breaking a rule that had never existed. When he had been trying to reach out, too. He wondered for half a second what would happen if he refused, if he put his bread in the toaster and stood there, staring at his father until smoke curled into the kitchen.

But he remembered what Uncle Becker had asked him to do, and what his mom had said while hugging him goodbye: *Don't forget your father didn't want this. I was the one who wanted to separate. You need to make things easy on him out there, okay?*

It was exactly like her to think of that. She always planned out everything—even the divorce. From the minute her mind was made up, she'd executed each detail with precision, even planning for how Jeremy's dad might feel out at the beach, trusting that Jeremy would take care of him.

Jeremy nodded once and headed for the bathroom to wash up.

A reply finally pinged into Jeremy's phone as Uncle Becker drove them into town:

Sounds good. Call if you need. Make sure you're getting some vegetables out there.

They stopped by the grocery store first. Jeremy's dad hadn't brought any sort of list, so the Ryden men shopped by feel, as Becker put it, filling the cart with cereal, milk, chips, bread, meat, fruit snacks, ice cream, popcorn, soda, wine, and, on the rack under the cart, a case of beer. Jeremy's dad always drank the same beer, Mason's, with the name running vertically down the side of the bottles. It was his thing.

Jeremy quietly threw in a few bags of pre-chopped vegetables as they passed the produce, and Becker laughed and messed up his hair again.

After stowing the cold things in a cooler in Uncle Becker's truck, the three of them walked a loop around the rest of Rosemont. It was a small town, neat as a postcard: a long strip of tourist shops, two bed-and-breakfasts, a handful of restaurants. Jeremy thought it was nice—tidy and safe-looking and predictable. Becker complained about the number of tourists. Jeremy's dad seemed bored.

They ate lunch at Sandy's Grill, where Becker made them sit at the tiled bar counter so he and Jeremy's dad could wrap the blond woman behind it in conversation. Her name tag identified her as Sandy herself, the manager and owner. Sandy had obviously known Becker a long time, and the majority of her smiles were directed at Jeremy's dad, who quickly began to smile back. Becker looked delighted.

When the lunch plates were cleared and both men had full glasses of beer in front of them, Jeremy, feeling brave, asked if he could go walk around town on his own.

"Oh, sorry, are we boring you?" said his father.

"Of course we're boring him!" Becker laughed. "Jer doesn't want to listen to us. He wants to get out and explore!"

"There *are* some really super stores here," Sandy said. She had beautiful cheekbones and rose-pink skin, with smile lines around her eyes and mouth. Jeremy decided he liked her. "There's Sharma's Rocks and Gems—they've got fossils. Keep your hands in sight, though; Mr. Sharma can be a bit suspicious of kids. Not that you're a kid!" She held up both palms. "I mean, look at you, almost a man!"

Jeremy's dad chuckled and lifted his beer. "Just be back in an hour if you want a ride home."

"I can probably walk back," said Jeremy, getting off his stool. "I know the way now."

"Suit yourself."

The grown-up chatter started again as Jeremy took a step toward the door. Back in Corvallis, this was the part where his mom would have asked if he had his key, and if his phone was charged, and if he needed any money. He did have money, thanks to her—she'd tucked an envelope of bills into his bag after hugging him goodbye, enough to make him catch his breath when he opened it later. And his cell phone was charged. He did have his key. But it looked like nobody else needed to know that. Not now. Not here. Not in this new sort of family.

He crossed the red-and-yellow carpets of Sandy's Grill alone and stepped out into the world.

The brightly painted buildings and chattering tourists expanded around him as he headed back toward the shops, feeling untethered and floaty. That shimmering feeling of possibility had returned, filling up the day.

There were people everywhere—families, little kids, clusters of loud teenagers—but Jeremy moved among them all without being noticed, happy and relieved to learn he could blend in here just as well as back home.

He made his first stop at Sharma's Rocks and Gems and discovered Sandy had been right: It was definitely worth a visit. They had pyrite and opals and bird skeletons, and fossilized shells trapped in slate, and geodes like dirty potatoes that you could buy and have cracked open with a special machine to see what kind of crystals were inside. Mr. Sharma, tall and bald, with golden-brown skin and a stylishly trimmed white beard, gave Jeremy an approving nod when he linked his arms behind his back and kept them there, admiring the displays like he was in the world's fanciest museum. Jeremy even got a smile when he bought himself a geode and a tiny bag of shark's teeth.

"Ready to open that geode, young man?" Mr. Sharma asked, handing over the receipt. "Remember, no refunds if it's mostly rock; there's no way to tell what's inside."

"Oh, no, thank you." Jeremy cradled the mottled stone egg in his hand. It had a satisfying, secure feel to it. "I think I want to wait. Can I bring it in sometime later, maybe?"

Mr. Sharma's forehead creased. "I suppose."

The bell tinkled as Jeremy stepped back into the street, where he immediately had to hop out of the way of a man wrangling a stroller and two excited dogs. The dogs barked at Jeremy, then at a pair of teenage girls skateboarding down the opposite sidewalk. Jeremy watched the girls until they passed a fancy-looking junk shop, which yanked his eyes to a dead stop. A sign above the window read

Tidepool Knickknacks. Jeremy's heart began thudding in his chest. He headed over.

The window display was packed, overflowing with vases, teacups, dolls, clocks, decorative knives, golf clubs, and a lifetime's worth of secondhand jewelry. Jeremy stood on tiptoe right up against the glass, then crouched, peering past the lace curtains and clutter, searching the shelves inside, hoping to find . . .

Yes, there in the back corner! A long, low shelf of magazines.

Jeremy's love for fashion magazines was his second-biggest secret, never shared with anyone, ever, not once. His hidden stash in Corvallis had been carefully cobbled together over the years from his mom's recycling bin, and he knew every one by heart from the long weekend afternoons he'd spent escaping into their glamorous pages. He'd even cut and pasted his very favorite photos into a scrapbook made from a leftover spiral notebook from school. Leafing through those highlights had helped him more than once when he was feeling down and lonely during the divorce. He didn't know all the technical terms of fashion, the language of fabrics and styles and clothes, but he knew when something reached out of the page and pressed a hand to his heart. He knew when something was too beautiful to let go.

On the drive in, he'd briefly considered starting a new scrapbook out here on the coast. He had the money from his mom, and all it would take was a few brave trips to a grocery store or gas station to get started. But the idea hadn't lasted long. What if he went in later with his dad and the attendant recognized the tall boy with freckles who bought fashion magazines? What if they said something?

This, right here, right now, might be his one perfect chance. There was no way his dad would ever set foot in Tidepool Knickknacks, and if Jeremy bought all their magazines in one trip, he'd never have to come back himself. His dad and Uncle Becker seemed pretty settled at Sandy's Grill, so he should have enough time to stock up and run everything home. He could hide the stash in his bedroom, smuggle it out in his bags when they left. No problem.

This was a once-in-a-summer opportunity.

The door groaned as he stepped inside, and Jeremy immediately felt like he'd fallen right through the glass into the window display. Too many things sat on too many shelves in the shop, stretching in uneven rows to the back, where an entire wall of frilly baby dresses hung beside an American flag and an old French horn. The place smelled musty. There were no other customers, but there was classical music playing, and a sparkly purple women's jacket was slung over a chair behind the cluttered counter.

"Hello?" Jeremy called. There was no answer.

He edged around a display of cookie tins and owl figurines and squeezed along the nearest aisle. He felt taller than normal in here, and extra awkward, like he had sixteen elbows and knees all working against one another. At last, he reached his goal, crouched down, and tilted his head to scan the shelves.

Most of the magazines were *National Geographic*, of course, followed by a long run of hunting and fishing magazines, the *New Yorker*, some cooking guides, and . . . yes! Yes! The delicate, cool *V* of *Vogue* rippled at him in waves from the last half foot of the row, along with a *Vanity Fair* or two squeezed in at the end. Jeremy grinned, sending a mental thank-you to his mom for the money, and reached out to pull the whole section free from the shelf and into his life.

"Can I help you?" said a man's voice.

Jeremy yelped and snatched his hands back, his sixteen elbows banging into his sixteen knees as he jerked around. He looked up, and his insides turned to flame, searing his throat and sending a wildfire blazing across his face.

It wasn't a man standing over him at all.

It was the runner boy from the beach.

Three

"Wh-what?" Jeremy said. He climbed unsteadily to his feet, three of his elbows bumping into shelves along the way.

"I said, can I help you?"

Runner Boy was wearing light gray jeans and a blue surfing company T-shirt. He was shorter than Jeremy. His dark hair was going shaggy, its waves breaking at the ends. His eyes were brown. There was a tiny dimple in his chin. He—

Jeremy realized he was staring.

"No! No help needed!" he said. "I was just looking at . . ." One of his hands gestured vaguely toward the shelf above the magazines. "Do you, um, work here?"

Runner Boy's eyes flicked to where Jeremy was gesturing. Jeremy looked over, too, seeing with a surge of relief that it contained an antique chain saw.

"I help out. This is my grandma's place. She's getting lunch."

"Cool!" Jeremy said, feeling anything but. "That's so cool!"

Runner Boy's eyebrows lifted slightly. "Well, if you need me . . ."

He headed back to the front, leaving Jeremy alone in the corner, his heart leaping so high it was bruising the roof of his mouth.

What now?

Obviously, he couldn't get the magazines anymore. It was bad enough he'd almost gotten caught looking at them. But he couldn't just run away without buying anything, either; that would look suspicious.

Jeremy drifted back among the aisles, scanning the shelves, stealing as many glimpses of Runner Boy as he dared.

He had to find something to buy. Anything.

Finally, he approached the counter, his palms sweating, and plonked down a set of salt and pepper shakers shaped like bald eagles.

"Not getting the chain saw?" Runner Boy asked.

Jeremy forced a laugh and did his best to sound like Becker, easygoing and relaxed. "Nah, just these. For my mom."

"Does she collect them or something?"

Nope. "Yup!"

Runner Boy peeled a sticker off the salt shaker and typed a number into the ancient cash register. His dark eyes zeroed in on Jeremy. "Your family here for vacation?"

"Yeah," Jeremy said. "Well, sort of. My dad and I are here for a bit because my mom— They're not— She's—" He was losing track of the question. "My parents just got divorced," he managed. "And we're here while my mom moves out of our old house."

"Oh, sorry. My parents are separated, too. That'll be eight fifty."

Jeremy fumbled for his wallet, hiding the thick band of bills. He didn't want to look like he was showing off. Why had he even brought so much? He should have left most of it at the house.

"How long's *a bit?*" asked Runner Boy. Jeremy looked up, blinking. "You said you and your dad were here for a bit. What's that mean?"

"Oh! Two weeks. From today. We're staying at one of my uncle's properties on the beach."

"Nice."

The orchestra played while Runner Boy took Jeremy's money and finished the sale, silently handing over the change.

"Must be rough," Jeremy said, "having to listen to this all day." He pointed up to indicate the music. "Does your grandma put it on?"

"I put it on." Runner Boy pulled open a drawer of tissue paper and began wrapping the shakers. "My grandma listens to oldies."

Jeremy could have kicked himself. He didn't really have thoughts about classical music one way or the other, but he'd guessed it was a safe thing to make fun of to try and seem cool. He'd guessed wrong.

"Awesome," said Jeremy, nodding hard as Runner Boy finished wrapping. The transaction was ending. He had seconds left. "Hey, so, I'm Jeremy, by the way." He waved a hand, instantly regretting the way his fingers curled through the air.

The touch of a smile, and maybe something like a question, appeared on Runner Boy's face. "Evan," he said.

Jeremy felt the name sink through him like sunshine. A muscle between his shoulder blades relaxed. *Evan.*

"How old are you?" Jeremy asked, pushing his luck.

"Thirteen in August. You?"

"Thirteen in December! And you live here?"

Evan shook his head. "With my mom in Newport. I do summers here to help my grandma during tourist season."

"Guess I'm a tourist, too, huh?"

"Yup."

"Hahaha!" Jeremy's laugh came out high and honking, and he looked away in horror. "Oh! Hey!" he said, spotting an escape. "I have that book! It was in my new room." He pointed to a battered copy of *Seabirds of the Central Oregon Coast* sitting behind the counter. "I got woken up today by a bunch of—hang on—Heermann's gulls? I think?"

"Oh, them. Yeah, they're loud. I always see them on the beach when I run."

Jeremy swallowed. "You run on the beach? That's cool."

Evan nodded, the waves in his dark hair shifting. "Most days. I run cross-country at school, so I try to keep my time up over break. There's not much else to do around here, anyway. The forts are usually taken in the summer, and there are too many grown-ups around town. But the beach goes on a long way."

"What are the *forts?*"

"You know, piles of driftwood you can go in. People build them into cabins where the logs get washed above the tide line. Little kids take them over during the day, but at night it's usually teenagers making out and stuff. Unless it's raining."

"Oh," Jeremy breathed.

"Yeah, it's annoying."

"They sound super, super awesome." Something alarming was happening to Jeremy's brain.

The door opened, letting in the sounds of the busy street and a group of white-haired old ladies.

"Hello, welcome," Evan called politely. The ladies greeted

him, exclaiming in happiness as they eased into the shop.

Jeremy wondered what he could say in the next ten seconds that might somehow keep this astonishing conversation going. He could almost feel his brain fizzing.

"Thanks for coming in," Evan said, sliding the wrapped shakers across the counter.

Jeremy's time was up.

"You too! I mean—thanks." He did not want to go, but he knew if he stood there one second longer, he would ruin absolutely everything. He headed for the door, trying to fumble the shakers into his pocket but somehow dislodging his geode instead. It hit the wood floor with a bang.

"You okay?" called Evan.

Jeremy scrambled after the rock. "Ha ha, yeah! I just dropped something I got at the fossil shop. I wasn't stealing, promise!"

One of the old ladies gave him a smile.

"Is that a geode?" asked Evan. A small frown appeared on his face. "Why didn't you get it cracked open? Isn't the whole point to find out what's inside?"

Jeremy glanced at the dull lump of stone in his hand. "I kind of like not knowing, I guess," he said. He curled his fingers around it. "It's like . . . holding on to a question I don't have to answer yet."

He glanced up, ready to be embarrassed, but Evan's frown was giving way to a surprised smile. Jeremy hesitated just long enough to feel his own smile widening in return, then fled the shop, emerging shaken, proud, and giddy into the noise and heat of the glorious summer afternoon.

Four

WEDNESDAY, JUNE 27

The Heermann's gulls woke Jeremy again the next morning, and he smiled into his pillow, remembering the knickknack shop. And Evan.

Evan with the wavy hair. Evan with the smile. Evan with the dimple in his chin. Evan with the calm, solid confidence. That may have been the most impressive thing. He'd talked to Jeremy like it was nothing, and to the group of old ladies, too. He'd talked like he wasn't scared of any of them, like he knew he would never embarrass himself or run out of things to say.

Jeremy wondered if he could become that confident someday. He doubted it.

Downstairs, he washed his face and hands, following the new rules to avoid making trouble, but his dad didn't even notice. Becker was already there, and they were talking over rock music blaring from the kitchen radio.

"Whatcha think, Jer?" Becker asked, waving a hand at the shiny aviator sunglasses perched on his brother's face. "Your old man look like the coolest dude in town?"

Jeremy couldn't think what to say, so he gave a small shrug and turned to the fridge.

"Ha!" Becker barked his laugh. "Moody preteen alert! Maybe I should get the kid a pair, too, now he's old enough to have an attitude."

"What he is," said Jeremy's dad, "is old enough to know better. And if Jeremy wants new sunglasses, he can buy them himself." He took off the aviators, setting them carefully on the kitchen counter. "Speaking of, what are you planning to do for money while we're here, Jeremy?"

Jeremy looked up from the cereal he was pouring. He was pretty sure telling his dad about the money his mom had given him would not be the best idea. More than once in the years before the split he'd heard his dad gripe about always being left out of her planning, left playing catch-up to her preemptive parenting choices. It seemed to really get under his skin.

Jeremy opted for the safety of another shrug.

His dad's face curved down, but Becker barked again. "Wish I could be that relaxed about money!" he said. "But seriously, lemme know if you need some, Jer. I've got plenty of chores that need doing around this place—gutters, dirty siding, washing bird poop off the roof. I'll pull a list together; just let me know what you charge."

"Oh, no," said Jeremy's dad before Jeremy could reply. "He'll work for free." He turned to his son. "Your uncle's giving us an amazing deal on this place, Jeremy, but I'm still paying. The least you can do is a few chores while we're here. I expect you to contribute, okay?"

Jeremy pulled in a breath, biting the inside of his cheek. This was . . . new.

His dad had always been the relaxed parent while he was growing up, the one who never fussed about rules and chores and expectations. The one who would tell Jeremy to quit halfway through mowing the lawn so they could play catch, or serve cold cereal and ice cream when it was his turn to make dinner, or help finish off Jeremy's homework so they could watch bad TV together on nights his mom got in late. His dad had always loved getting away with things, loved rebelling against what people expected from a fortysomething college professor and father.

But he'd changed during the slow grind of the divorce, turning more serious, spending less time with Jeremy, giving up his old displays of fun, and he seemed to be doubling down on that here on the coast. Was he trying to level up his parenting? Act more like Jeremy's mom somehow by dishing out orders and making up rules? It almost felt like he saw Jeremy as some sort of problem kid or stranger now. Like without knowing why, Jeremy had lost his dad's trust.

Whatever was happening, Jeremy could tell he wouldn't get anywhere by trying to argue. He nodded and left, taking his breakfast with him, just catching a wink from Uncle Becker as he headed up the stairs.

He spent the rest of the morning in his room away from the confusing grown-ups, sitting cross-legged on his bed beside the window, scanning the beach every few minutes for a flash of red shorts—just in case—and flipping through the bird book.

Horned grebe.

Those were the small black-and-white birds wandering in a clump down by the tide line.

Snowy plover.

Soft brown-and-cream-colored birds, trotting around on stilt legs. He'd spotted some of those scavenging in the sand that morning? Maybe?

Osprey.

He definitely hadn't seen one of those yet, with their bright white undersides, curved beaks, and speckled wings. The guide said they had *outstanding environmental adaptability,* since they were strong hunters that were just as happy catching rodents and smaller birds inland as they were diving for fish along the coast.

Jeremy set the book down and leaned his head against the frame. *Environmental adaptability.* That sounded pretty nice. Being able to take care of yourself no matter where you ended up? The skills to stay happy however much things changed? He could use some of that in his own life for sure. It would probably make living with his dad easier— for the summer or forever, depending on how his decision went.

The morning rolled on into a sweltering afternoon, and by lunchtime, the attic room had become hot and stuffy. Jeremy was lying on his back on the floor when his phone pinged, interrupting another dreamy replay of his conversation with Evan. He crawled over. A text from his mom had gotten through.

Hey, please call asap. Not emergency! Just time we talked!

He tapped the screen to dial her number and turn on speaker-phone, but the network only stared blankly at him, refusing to reconnect. He sighed. Calling her back would probably require walking all the way into town. But at least that would be an excuse not to start any chores today, an excuse his dad couldn't argue with. And while he was in town, well, who knew who he might happen to bump into?

The sidewalks of Rosemont were not, it turned out, the greatest place in the world to make a phone call. After having to ask his mom to repeat herself three times, Jeremy ducked down a side street, just far enough away from the crowds, shops, and cars of Main Street to hear.

"Okay," he said. "Sorry. I'm here."

"That's much better, isn't it, honey?" said his mom. "Well, what I was saying was I found the most amazing Shakespeare festival happening here! They've got sword-fighting lessons and everything. You're interested in Shakespeare, aren't you? I've bought tickets and added it to our calendar for your first visit. The Beaverton City Library I think we can save for your second trip, though it does look very nice and I think we should see it together. Oh, and of course there's the Night Market! That's in August, so we'll have to decide how to fit that into your stay here then."

Jeremy listened, smiling a little, as his mom went through a list of items she had clearly prepared ahead of time for their chat. A black-and-yellow butterfly flitted by, and he began ambling after it, enjoying the quiet of the narrow street and the shade of its tall buildings.

"Now, I haven't started prepping your room yet," his mom continued. "I've got so many other details to handle before I start work after the Fourth. It is beyond inconvenient it falls on a Wednesday this year! Everyone seems ready to turn the whole week into an extra-long weekend, and settling times and dates with the movers has turned into a real headache. But I don't want you to worry, love! The house will be all set up, and your room will be perfect when you come to stay. I'll take care of it."

Jeremy didn't feel quite ready to talk about his visits to Beaverton later in the summer, seeing as he was only just getting settled in on the coast. He made a sound of general agreement and let his mom go on, changing topics to tell him all about her new office and the farmers' market that set up every Friday right there in the parking lot.

"And how are you, honey?" his mom asked when she was finally done with her list. "Your text said you got the attic room? How is that? Do you have two ways out in case of fire?"

Jeremy mimed a check mark in the air with his finger. "Yep," he said. "The window leads to the porch roof, so I can always climb down if I need to."

His mom made a worried noise. "That sounds dangerous, sweetie, climbing down off a roof?"

"It's really fine, Mom."

"And if you can climb down, then does that mean someone else could climb up? Jeremy, I want you to be sure you're locking your window securely each night."

"I will, Mom."

"Double-check for me."

"I will."

"And your uncle is there enough helping out? Making sure you two are okay? Is he the closest neighbor you could run to if you needed help?"

Jeremy resisted the urge to roll his eyes as the black-and-yellow butterfly passed him again, going back the other way. He was used to his mom's need to plan for the worst and dig into every detail, but she didn't usually save everything up and unleash it all at once like this.

"Uncle Becker lives in town," he answered. "But yeah, there are other beach houses close to us. I'll be fine, Mom, I promise."

"I trust you, Jeremy. It's just knowing you're there alone with your father and his brother that gets me worried." She let out a long breath. "Anyway, how are things going overall? Is the ocean everything you hoped for? What are you doing with your time?"

Jeremy scanned his memories of the last two days. He knew better than to tell his mom he was roaming the streets of Rosemont by himself, or bring up how his dad was acting differently out here, and he wasn't ready to tell anyone in the world about the amazing conversation with Evan. So instead, he told her all about the beach, and his visit to Sharma's Rocks and Gems, and the names of the local seabirds he was learning from his book.

"Oh, honey, I'm so proud," his mom said when he finished. "It sounds like you're really making the most productive use you can out of your time down there. I wouldn't expect anything less, but I'm still so happy to hear it." A chime sounded from her side of things, followed by the sudden tapping of a keyboard. "Love, I've got to run," she said. "I'm so glad we got to talk. Let's do it again in the next few days. And just to triple-check, you've got everything you need? And you're doing all right?"

"Yes, Mom."

"Well, I'll say goodbye, then, honey. Stay safe! I love you!"

"Love you, too."

"Don't forget to wear sunscreen!" she added, barely finishing the word before she ended the call.

Jeremy let out a long, long breath, blowing out his cheeks and closing his eyes. Then he opened them again and looked around, wondering what to do next.

He would need some lunch eventually, but he could always wander Rosemont a bit first, just to make sure he knew his way around. Maybe in the general direction of some of the shops? Maybe in the general direction of Tidepool Knickknacks?

He took two steps, then stopped short. What on earth was he thinking? He couldn't go in *every* day and say he was buying a present for his mom. That would look suspicious. He would have to pace himself. He would have to be patient.

He was turning back toward the main road, thinking vaguely of the nearby sandwich place, when a door opened in one of the buildings and an old woman in a butter-yellow sweat suit stepped out, followed closely by . . . Evan.

The woman was short. She had spiky gray hair and a dark, wrinkly tan. Bright pink flowers ran down the arms and legs of her sweat suit. She and Evan were laughing.

Jeremy stood, frozen. Even from a distance, he saw that laughing gave Evan dimples.

Neither of them had spotted Jeremy, and as they walked off in the opposite direction, he began silently freaking out. Evan was there! Right there! Jeremy had daydreamed about running into him, sure, but he'd never thought it would actually happen. Only it had! This was his chance! His chance to say hi, to talk again without it being suspicious. Maybe the only chance he would get!

He squeezed his eyes shut. He could do this. He could make a friend in the in-between. He could be cool.

"Evan!"

The shout echoed around the street, sending three pigeons and a seagull flapping away. Evan and the old woman stopped and looked behind them.

"Oh, hey. Jeremy, right?"

Jeremy stayed rooted to the spot. He hadn't mean to yell that loudly.

"How's it going?" Evan called.

Jeremy considered making a run for it. He could lose himself among the tourists, forget about lunch, and go back to hiding in his room for the next two weeks, living off toast and rainwater and soul-crushing embarrassment.

Evan and the old lady walked over to join him. "What are you doing back here?" Evan asked. "Are you lost?"

"No! Ha!" Jeremy managed. "I had to, um, make a call." He waggled his phone in the air as proof, then immediately wished he hadn't. "It was quieter here, so . . . how about you?"

Evan pointed over his shoulder. "That's our back door."

"Wait, to the shop?" How had he not realized he was so close?

"And my grandma's place; she lives above it. Me too when I'm here."

"And speaking of *your grandma*," the old lady said loudly. She'd been looking back and forth between them as they talked, her eyebrows getting higher and higher.

"Oh, sorry," Evan said. "Grandma, this is Jeremy. Jeremy, this is my grandma."

Jeremy held out a hand. "Nice to meet you, Ms. . . ."

"Gloria, honey, please! Call me Gloria!" The old lady seized his hand in a firm grip. "It's always gorgeous to meet a friend of Evan's. And aren't you just a cutie! Are you here for the summer? Are you staying in town?"

"No. I mean yeah!" said Jeremy. Gloria was completely overwhelming. "I mean—I'm staying at a place on the beach for a couple weeks. With my dad."

"Lucky you!" Gloria squeezed Jeremy's arm. "Evan runs on the beach! Did he tell you? Maybe you've seen him go by?"

Jeremy felt himself turning several shades of red at once. "I haven't, but he did—he did tell me. About the running."

"You should take Jeremy with you!" Gloria backhanded Evan across the chest. "Show your new friend around! Make sure he falls in love with the place!"

"Sure," said Evan. "But, hey, we gotta get going." He turned to Jeremy. "Sorry, one of Grandma's friends is covering the shop so we can grab lunch. Here." He held out a hand. "Let me give you my number."

Time slowed to an underwater crawl as Jeremy handed over his phone and watched, barely breathing, as Evan tapped at it.

"You're good." Evan passed the phone back. "Text me later so I've got yours."

"It was very, very nice meeting you, honey," said Gloria. She pulled Jeremy into a hug before he could do anything more than open and close his mouth. "I hope to see you again soon. You enjoy this beautiful day!"

"Bye, dude," called Evan, waving as the two of them headed down the street.

Jeremy stood, still holding his phone in his outstretched hand, until they turned the corner and disappeared.

He wondered if he would ever understand what had just happened. He'd barely spoken ten words, and most of them were nonsense. Yet somehow, he'd ended up with Evan's number. And an invitation to text. And a possible running date.

Wonder shivered through Jeremy's body. Everything in his experience up till now told him life just wasn't like this. It couldn't be. Not for him.

Only it looked like when it came to this summer, and the in-between, and Evan . . . maybe it was.

Five

Uncle Becker came by the house again that evening and made them all dinner, setting up a taco bar in the kitchen and cracking a bottle of tequila for the grown-ups. Jeremy's dad had spent the day making a big show of his college-professor paperwork, burying the dining room table under folders and stacks of textbooks in the process, so they ate out on the porch. The two men claimed the rocking chairs; Jeremy returned to his spot on the railing.

The brothers talked while they ate, settling into an easy rhythm of competition and insults they'd clearly been perfecting since they were young. Jeremy didn't listen. He was busy thinking about the number waiting in his phone under the name *Evan Sandford*.

He hadn't tried texting Evan yet. He wanted to swim in the anticipation for just a little longer. He wanted to stay giddy. He wanted to memorize this feeling of butterflies.

"Oy, Jer!"

Jeremy snapped his head around. His dad and Becker were looking at him.

"Huh?"

"I said, *how was your day?*" Becker took a slurp of his margarita. "Man, you are out of it. You fall in love or something?"

Jeremy felt his ears flush and fought down a wild urge to laugh. He coughed instead. "No, no. I got to see more of the town, though."

Becker raised his glass. "Right on. What do you think of the place?"

"It's nice," Jeremy said. "Really nice." He was not about to tell his dad and uncle about meeting Evan, and especially not about the feelings filling his insides over his new friend. But something pushed him to be just the tiniest bit daring. "I, um, found a store I liked."

"Yeah? Which one?"

"Tidepool Knickknacks?"

Becker grunted. "Never been in there."

Jeremy's dad, clearly bored, kicked Becker in the leg, pulling him into an argument about something from his college years.

Jeremy finished eating and headed in, piling his dishes in the sink for later like always. He turned to walk away, then stopped, thinking. The kitchen was already a mess, and Uncle Becker was over, and his dad was drinking again . . .

He turned back to the sink. They hadn't talked about who was going to be in charge of this sort of thing during their stay, but given what he'd seen so far, there was a 100 percent chance his dad would call him down to clean it up. He might as well get ahead of the game. He sure didn't want to be interrupted once he'd texted Evan.

He put away the taco shells and wilty shredded lettuce, scrubbed the piled greasy plates, and wiped salsa from the counters. The next two weeks would probably be easier if he just did things like this without being asked, he decided, squeezing out the sponge. His dad probably wouldn't notice, but it should smooth out their stay. That was the whole goal of *environmental adaptability*, right?

Two minutes after the last dish was finished, Jeremy was leaning against his bedroom window, early sunset light glowing on the walls, cradling his phone in his soapsud-scented hands. He'd waited as long as he could stand; it was time to text Evan.

Well, try to text Evan. It was up to the universe if whatever he sent would actually get through.

His heart playing jump rope with his stomach, he pulled up the number, tapped the text icon . . . and found himself utterly frozen.

What in the entire earth and sky and ocean were you supposed to say to someone you'd just met and wanted to get to know?

> Hello, this is Jeremy from earlier. Would you like to be friends?

> Hi! Jeremy here! How's it going new buddy?

> I am Jeremy. Hang out with me.

> Thanks for your number. Here's mine. It's Jeremy btw. We already met.

Everything his brain suggested was a disaster. The minutes ticked by. Draft after draft got erased before it was halfway typed. Jeremy stared out the window. A moth was battering against the glass. His dad's and uncle's laughter echoed up from the porch.

He shook his head. *Come on! Just send something!* His fingers moved, and words appeared on the screen.

> Hey, it's that Jeremy kid. Hope your day was good! Thanks for being nice.

He hit send before he could stop himself. Then he swallowed and brought the phone right up to his nose.

Oh, screaming seagulls. That was the worst text yet.

He flung himself onto his bed, groaning into the blankets. Why, why, why, why, *why* did he have to be so bad at this?

The only consolation came from their terrible reception. Evan probably wouldn't even get the text for hours, and Jeremy wouldn't have to see a reply—or lack of a reply, more likely—until the next time he went into town. Which, based on how he was feeling, would be just about never.

The men on the porch laughed again, louder, wilder, sounding very full of tequila. The moth thumped against the window. He could hear waves through the walls of the house.

From its spot half-buried under his pillow, his phone gave a ping.

Jeremy lifted his head. He blinked, and so did the light indicating a text. He heard another ping, then another.

He sat up.

Someone was texting him. And the texts were getting through.

Moving like someone approaching a very dangerous animal, Jeremy reached for the phone. He held it up, staring at the screen.

He had three new messages waiting. Three.

They were all from Evan.

Six

It was a miracle. It had to be. How else could Evan's texts be finding their way through whatever fog bank of reception the beach house was lurking in?

He thumbed open the three waiting messages.

Hey Jeremy

No problem you too

What's up?

Jeremy had to reread his own embarrassing text to put the replies in context. His face went hot, and he stared at the eight precious words from Evan. Obviously he had to write back now, but saying what? Should he start with how amazingly incredible it was that Evan's texts were reaching him? Probably not. He didn't want to come across as overwhelming.

Not much, he typed, his tongue between his teeth in concentration.

Had dinner with my dad and uncle. I'm hanging out in my room now.

He read it over three times before sending, bracing himself for the spinning wheel, but the text blipped into place immediately. His screen was still glowing when the reply came in.

That's cool

Jeremy rearranged himself so he was sitting cross-legged, holding his phone in front of him like a model airplane before the glue had dried. Okay, okay, this was good. But what now? Was he supposed to go next? What on earth should he say?

You like it here so far?

Jeremy had never been so grateful to be asked a question in his life. He replied almost without thinking.

Yeah! You?

Ugh, why did he just throw it back like that? He didn't want to mess this up. Every text mattered.

Can be kinda boring. But it's ok

The beach is better when people are gone

Okay, the beach, they could talk about the beach. He started typing.

Somehow, slowly, a whole conversation happened. Jeremy sent out his careful messages, and Evan flung back one-line replies almost instantly. Jeremy was floored. He was agonizing over every word, over every second he took to gather his thoughts, stressing about spelling and tone and accidental hidden meanings in his punctuation. Evan didn't seem to be doing any of that. Evan seemed to feel comfortable saying whatever crossed his mind. Jeremy couldn't imagine what that must be like.

They talked about the beach at first, then the town, the weather, recent movies only one of them had seen. Evan mentioned a visit to Hawaii over winter break, and Jeremy shared a string of texts about visiting the redwoods in Northern California. Every time things seemed to be winding down, Jeremy would pull out another topic at the last second, or Evan would ask another question. When Jeremy glanced up, grinning, from an especially long Evan text—nineteen whole words!—he was surprised to discover it was fully dark outside. Night had fallen, and his room was a cave of golden light from the lamp on his bedside table.

The bird book was sitting under the lamp, and he snatched it up, remembering.

> I saw some more birds today by the way. There were lots of marbled murrelets down by the water when we were eating dinner.

> Oh yeah, they're like the bird of summer. Everyone says they're friendly

> Friendly seabirds? What does that mean?

> No idea

> I've got the guidebook here, the same one you had at your shop. Wait a second.

Jeremy cracked the book open, his heart fluttering as he flipped through the pages. Nerves or not, this was going really, really well. He found the proper page and scanned it.

Okay, you won't believe this.

What

It even says in the book that they're friendly. They like being around other groups of birds and they're not scared of people.

Weird. So marbled murrelets = friends?

A delicate shiver tingled across the back of Jeremy's neck. His fingers flew as he took the ball and ran with it.

Yes! That's awesome! What would Heermann's gulls equal, then?

Noisy

Annoying

Interrupting

Screaming

Haha! There could be a whole secret language using birds.

Right

Hey what are you doing tomorrow

Jeremy, hunched over the book, almost fell forward onto his face.
Casual! He had to sound casual. He tried to imitate Evan's easygoing tone.

Dunno yet. Might check out the beach some more.
See the rest of town.

Yes, good. That was good.

We could go running, like my grandma said

Do you like to run?

Jeremy had no idea. He'd never tried outside gym class.

Yes. Definitely.

Cool. Where on the beach is your place?

His heart clomping all around his ribs, Jeremy described the
house and its exact location.

Oh nice I run that way a lot. I'll swing by

Jeremy said the word out loud as he typed it: "Yes."

Is 2 ok? I'm working in morning

That's perfect!

He stopped, suddenly picturing Evan up on the porch, forced to shake hands with his dad. His insides squirmed at the thought. He wanted to keep his dad and uncle far away from whatever this was he'd found here. He wanted to keep Evan all to himself.

> Hey, can we actually meet a little past my place? At that giant log with its roots pointing at the water, maybe?

He chewed his lip, worried Evan would want an explanation. But relief washed through him at the reply.

> Cool. See you then!

It was the first exclamation mark Evan had used. Jeremy forced himself to keep it together for one more text.

> See you then. G'night!

Jeremy dropped his phone and collapsed back onto the pillows.

Downstairs, his dad and Uncle Becker had put on some sort of arena rock. Dramatic wailing and electric guitars rumbled through the floor as Jeremy drummed his hands and feet into his mattress in pure happiness.

He'd had a whole conversation with Evan! He'd become actual friends with Evan! He was going to go running with Evan! He was going . . .

He sat bolt upright.

He was going to have to find himself some running shoes.

Seven

THURSDAY, JUNE 28

The next morning Jeremy faced two genuine, earth-shaking problems: He had no idea where in town he could buy running shoes, and no idea who to ask to find out.

Uncle Becker might have known, but he was off doing maintenance on one of his other properties. His dad probably could have helped, but that would mean telling him why he wanted to know, which would have meant spilling the beans about the money. Besides, Jeremy was avoiding his dad as much as possible while the threat of chores was still hovering. He was not about to miss a run with Evan because he'd gotten cornered into scraping bird poop off the roof.

Texting Evan would have been the obvious solution, but that was out, since Jeremy had let it sound like running was something he already did. Admitting he didn't even have shoes yet would mean owning up to the lie.

With all other options off the table and two o'clock ticking nearer and nearer, he decided to head into town on his own, every dollar his mom had given him stuffed into his wallet, and hope for the best.

It was a beautiful day. The air was cool and sweet, and clusters of small brown birds—sparrows, maybe, or chickadees?—peeped from the tangles of blackberry and buttercup overflowing the roadside ditches. A line of old women rode by on motorcycles, all wearing American flag bandannas like an early Fourth of July parade. Every last one of them gave Jeremy a wave.

Passing the invisible cell coverage barrier brought in a few bars of service, enough for Jeremy to plug in a shoe-store search on his phone. But as he neared Main Street, his network suddenly folded up and surrendered, and the glowing wheel spun and spun, getting nowhere. He paced the sidewalk, waiting, then went to ask the only other person in town he could think of.

The door of Sharma's Rocks and Gems chimed gently as he stepped inside. Mr. Sharma was already busy, talking with two old white ladies in practical sun hats and hiking boots. Streaks of sunscreen shone on their bare arms and the backs of their necks, and they were giving Mr. Sharma a detailed account of the different stones and minerals they'd seen on a recent trip to the Grand Canyon. One of them kept waving a pair of trekking poles, and Mr. Sharma kept wincing as they whooshed past a glimmering three-foot-high amethyst and a display of fossilized fish.

Jeremy hovered by the entrance, remembering to put his hands behind his back, enjoying the clean, dry smell of the store's air-conditioning and wood counters. He'd intended to stay put so

Mr. Sharma would understand he wasn't taking advantage of the distraction to go around stealing things, but the ladies talked so long that he'd inched halfway to the back out of sheer boredom by the time they were done.

The door chimed again as the ladies left, and Mr. Sharma turned to Jeremy with a look of relief. "Thirty minutes of my life those two took," he said. "And they didn't buy a thing." He shook his head and strode over. "I'm guessing you're here to crack open that geode, young man?"

Jeremy blinked. Mr. Sharma remembered him? Then he realized it probably wasn't normal behavior to buy a geode and not open it. He gulped.

"Not—not yet, thanks," he said. "I was, um, actually wondering if you maybe knew somewhere I could buy some running shoes?"

The smile hovering around Mr. Sharma's face dropped. "You came in to ask me how to find another type of shop?"

Jeremy gulped again. "And, um"—he looked around—"and because I need some of this." He reached for a random basket at his elbow and plucked out a small, clear amber-yellow rock. It looked like a chunk of crystalized honey.

"Citrine?" Mr. Sharma's eyebrows rose, then descended almost to his cheekbones. They stayed there. "You *need* a piece of citrine?"

"Um, yes?" Jeremy said, walking sideways to the counter. This was not going well at all. "But I also do need shoes, so if you could maybe point me toward a place to get some? I'd really, really appreciate it."

"What's wrong with the shoes you're wearing?"

"They're not for running."

"Ah. And you want to go running for some reason." Mr. Sharma sighed. "Well, I suppose you did buy something—that'll be three dollars, by the way. I can tell you how to find your store."

He took Jeremy's money and gave him directions, starting with where to board the local bus and ending with turning left once he'd walked past the drive-in. Ten minutes later, Jeremy was climbing onto a vinyl-scented seat, the citrine in his pocket and butterflies in his stomach over his first solo bus adventure ever. As the engine chugged onto the highway, he realized no one else in the world had any idea where he was or what he was doing. His dad wouldn't have cared, probably, but his mom would have completely freaked out if she'd known. He felt a little guilty realizing that. But also, strangely, a little good.

The views of the coast outside the bus window were very distracting, but Jeremy managed to get off at the proper stop, walk past the drive-in, turn left, and finally step through a pair of sliding glass doors into the cool red-and-white interior of the local Target.

Jeremy had never gone clothes shopping on his own before, and he'd definitely never had the money to buy whatever he wanted. He started by picking out two new heather-gray T-shirts and two pairs of running shorts—blue, in a shade that would look good beside Evan's red ones. Then he braced himself to tackle the mountain of options in the shoe department.

A nice lady in a red vest stopped by to ask if he needed any help, but Jeremy smiled her away and set to work on his own. He knew more or less what he needed, but there were so many factors to consider. He wanted shoes that looked nice, because of course, but not so nice he would feel bad about messing them up on the beach. He wanted cool shoes Evan would like, but not so cool it would look like he was showing off. He wanted shoes that said he was a runner who knew what he was doing, but not so technical they would be hard on his beginner's feet.

It was a tricky balance, and Jeremy was determined to get it right.

In the end, he left the checkout feeling almost completely good about his choice. The shoes he'd picked had taken a major chunk of the money from his mom, but when he'd tried to talk himself into a simpler, less expensive pair, he just hadn't been able to do it. He was all-in now on this chance for friendship with Evan, and buying the perfect shoes felt like making a commitment. From now on, running was going to be his thing. He almost felt like starting right then as he stepped out of the Target into the hot summer air.

He pulled the shoes out again at the bus stop bench, going over their soft padding, pristine tread, and perfect stitching in the sunlight. Deciding all at once, he kicked off his old shoes and pulled on the new ones, smiling at the way they wrapped around his feet like a hug. He would wear them part of the way home, he decided, just to get to know them. Just to break them in.

The bus arrived with a hiss of brakes, and he climbed on with a handful of other shoppers, snagging a window seat near the front. His new shoes glowed up at him from the floor, and as the bus pulled away, a bright, hopeful happiness rippled through him like the break-ers he could see through his window, tumbling proudly in to shore from the open, shining sea.

It was just after noon when Jeremy got back to the beach house. His dad was busy eating nachos and watching shark videos on his laptop, so Jeremy was able to smuggle in his Target bag before hurriedly making his own lunch and escaping to the safety of his room.

The next hour and a half crawled by, and by a quarter to two, he was already out at the big log just south of the house, tugging at his new T-shirt and bouncing nervously from foot to foot in the soft sand. His dad had only grunted when Jeremy told him he was going out for a run, apparently totally unaware this was a whole new thing in his son's life. He hadn't even noticed the fresh clothes.

Evan had texted to say they should leave their phones at home, since beach runs were an easy way to ruin them, so the minutes ticked along uncounted. Jeremy paced, feeling almost sick, until at long last Evan's red shorts appeared up the beach. Jeremy waved with both hands, realizing with a sweet zing of joy that it was safe to keep his eyes glued to Evan this time. He was just watching his new friend arrive. That was all.

"How's it going?" Evan asked as he came to a stop. "Hey, nice shoes." He pointed at Jeremy's feet. "Wish I had a pair like that!"

Jeremy looked down. "Really?" His voice cracked on the second syllable. "They were a present . . . from my mom." It wasn't exactly a lie; she had provided the money.

"Those are, like, *really* nice. Brand-new, too?"

Jeremy nodded. He could have kicked himself with his really nice, brand-new shoes. He'd bought the wrong pair. He should have gone for something more discreet. Hopefully they'd get scuffed up enough that Evan would forget.

"So, you ready?" Evan asked.

Jeremy gave a thumbs-up, bouncing on his toes again as Evan started off, heading south at an easy jog. Jeremy pulled in a deep breath and followed, feeling wildly self-conscious, his new blue shorts rubbing together and his feet rising and falling under him like bricks. When they reached the broad flat of the damp sand, Evan picked up the pace, and the real run began.

Jeremy quickly learned that he didn't like running. He'd been picturing the two of them loping easily along a quiet beach, the blue sky arcing dramatically above and the sun shining like a chandelier over the sea. They would talk about everything and nothing, and Jeremy would make Evan laugh, and Evan would demand they run together every day from then on, just the two of them. Everything would be perfect.

The reality turned out to be anything but. For starters, the wind roaring in from the ocean made it impossible to hear anything under a full shout. Not that Jeremy could have talked while he was panting with every breath. The glaring sun beat mercilessly on the top of his head, and the knots of tourists crowding the beach meant he and Evan had to keep shifting up and down from the wet, smushy tide line to the slippery dry sand and back. Jeremy's knees began to hurt. His eyes watered. His nose wouldn't stop running.

The really nice, brand-new shoes wasted no time raising blisters on Jeremy's heels, and within five minutes of setting out, his lungs felt like they'd been scoured with roofing tiles. Evan glanced over a few times, shooting him a half grin, which only kept Jeremy painfully aware of the sweat pouring down his face and his sixteen awkward, flailing hands.

The crowds of vacationers thinned as they went, then finally vanished. That brought some relief, at least, since Jeremy knew for certain every pair of eyes they'd passed had been trained on him, judging. The open beach held birds instead of people, whole flocks of them. They rose from the sand as the two boys passed, wheeling overhead, their cries masking Jeremy's own hoarse wheezing.

At last, as they rounded a bend into a shallow cove, Evan angled their path toward a heap of piled driftwood, and they came to a stop.

"How far", Jeremy panted, his hands on his knees, "did we—go?" They must have run half the Oregon coastline. The California border was probably just past the next curve.

"A bit under two miles." Evan leaned against the driftwood, breathing hard but comfortably.

"Under—two—miles?" Jeremy heaved himself upright. He opened his mouth to say how impossible that was, but then two things stopped him. The first was his brain's reaction to the sight of Evan.

Jeremy had once seen a semitruck stall, jerking to a stop in the middle of the street, and his nervous system went through a similar maneuver now. Evan was standing with one hand braced on a jutting branch of driftwood, his torso at an angle, the other hand pushing his hair off his face. Sunlight poured around him. His eyelashes cast long shadows over his cheekbones.

Lights swam across Jeremy's vision, and he felt the words he'd been about to say disappear like sea-foam on the wind. Which didn't turn out to matter, seeing as the second thing that happened was a sudden violent rebellion from the rest of his exhausted body that made him lurch forward, hunch back over his knees, point his sweating face at the sand, and throw up.

Eight

"Aw, buddy!"

Jeremy heard the words over his own horrible retching. A hand patted his back. "No worries. It's pretty common for new runners. Especially when they push too hard. You'll be okay."

The heaving eased, then ended, but Jeremy stayed crouched over, his nose and mouth dripping, his eyes fixed ahead of him on the unspattered sand. There sure were a lot of things in it: scraggly feathers, dried kelp, bits of Styrofoam, dead crabs. Maybe he could just stay there, staring at the collage they made forever. He spat again as Evan patted him on the back once more and stepped away.

"Hey, check it out, horned grebes."

Jeremy half raised his head. Evan was pointing to a nearby flock of birds. Jeremy wiped his mouth on his arm and stretched back up, his stomach giving one angry, cramping stab, then quieting. He squinted. "I think those are killdeers." His voice sounded like he'd eaten a handful of sand. "I mean, aren't they? From the tails?"

"Oh, so tourist guy spends a couple days on the coast and suddenly he's an expert?"

Jeremy tried to huff a laugh.

"The book'll prove me right," Evan said, smiling and raising his palms. "But, hey, remember that code thing? *Friends* bird and *annoying* bird? Keep that going. What should these ones mean?"

"Feeling awful."

That earned Jeremy a grin. He staggered over to sit on the drift-wood heap as Evan picked up a rock and lobbed it out to sea. A quiet minute passed, then another, and Jeremy realized that Evan, after gently distracting him, was letting him decide how much time he needed to recover.

This was a seriously epic disaster, of course. Evan was being nice, but Jeremy knew he'd ruined everything. He must have. He wiped at the snot and sweat streaking his face and spat again, trying to get the sour taste out of his mouth.

Finally, he broke the silence. "How'd you know I've never actually run before?" he asked. He could smell his own breath over the tang of the sea.

Evan had gathered a handful of shells and was crouched on the sand, looking them over one by one. "Easy tells," he answered. "Brand-new shoes, messy form, and, well, you know . . ."

"Throwing up," Jeremy finished. "Yeah, you caught me."

"So, why'd you say you like running, then?"

The answer roared like the wind in Jeremy's mind. He was surprised Evan couldn't see it in the air all around them.

Because I wanted to get closer to you.

"It seemed like fun, I guess?" Jeremy didn't want to lie again, but it wasn't as if he could just blurt out the truth. "You know, being outside, letting off steam, getting exercise and all that." Ugh, he was sounding like some weird combination of his parents. "Why are you into running?"

Evan shrugged. "For me, it's kind of like being in a story. There's a start and a stop, and the whole time in between you're in this other world or something, and everything else is just passing by." He looked out at the waves. "It's like when I run, I can, you know, slip between the cracks or whatever. To a place where I'm in charge. Life's happening on my time. Just for me."

"Whoa," said Jeremy. "It sounds really great when you say it like that. You run at school, too, right?"

Evan nodded. "Cross-country, mostly."

"So, you probably have a bunch of running friends?"

Evan looked down, responding after a long moment with a brief half shrug.

Jeremy instantly felt awful. He shouldn't have asked the question. He just kept messing things up.

Evan dropped the last shell and brushed off his hands. "So." He tilted his head at Jeremy. "You want to give running another go?"

Jeremy winced. "Honestly, I don't think—"

"No, no, I don't mean right now," said Evan, a smile sidling onto his face. "We're walking back today, for sure. But tomorrow, maybe, if you want? We can take it slow."

Jeremy felt a jolt of relief so strong it was like missing a step going downstairs. So he hadn't ruined everything after all? Evan still wanted to hang out? It was a marvel. Another one.

"Jeremy?"

He came back to himself. "Yes, yes! That'd be awesome. Running tomorrow. Yes."

"Cool." Evan stood, brushing sand off more places. "Ready to go, then? Tide's almost all the way out. We can walk along the water and look for washed-up jellyfish."

"Okay."

"And don't forget—we're checking that bird book back at your place. Bet you five bucks I was right."

Jeremy raised his palms like Evan had. "They were totally killdeer," he said. "And you're on." He remembered as he said it that he didn't want Evan getting anywhere near his dad, but it was too late to back out now. He'd just have to come up with a plan when they got there.

They didn't see any jellyfish as they walked along the waterline, but Jeremy did find plenty of weird rocks and shells, along with a lump of beach glass. It had been clear once, but the waves and scrubbing sand had turned it a frosted, milky white.

"You should keep that," said Evan. "Help you remember your first run."

Jeremy grimaced. "Like I could ever forget." But he let Evan get ahead, then tucked the glass into the pocket on his shorts, closing the Velcro over it.

"You're probably sick of shells and beach glass and stuff, aren't you?" he asked after a stretch of silence. It was a weird thing to say, but now they were walking, he felt a jittery need to keep up a conversation. "You know, from coming here every summer?"

Evan turned and quirked an eyebrow. "I don't know if shells are something you can get sick of," he said. "And I used to collect beach glass when I was little. Only the green, though. I still have it all somewhere."

"Is green your favorite color?" It was a total kindergarten question, but Jeremy had to know.

"Not anymore."

"What is, then?"

"Haven't decided." Evan turned so he was walking backward, facing Jeremy. "How about you?"

"Turquoise."

"Ha! You're definite about that!"

"I guess . . ." Jeremy had told the truth without meaning to.

"You don't see much turquoise beach glass. Don't know if I've seen *any*."

"I'll survive?"

Evan's smile widened. "I'll keep an eye out anyway."

Jeremy had to fake a coughing fit to hide his scarlet face.

It took them almost an hour to amble back, finally climbing together up the steps onto Jeremy's porch. Jeremy, his guard up since the beach house had come into sight, poked his head inside. His dad's laptop was sitting open on the table, the screen dark, with books and papers spread all around it. The house was silent.

"Dad?" he called softly. There was no reply. "Wait here," he whispered to Evan, then eased past the door and into the house.

The blinds on the living room window were drawn tight, but there was enough light to show Jeremy's father stretched out on the sofa, a blanket covering one shoulder. He was fast asleep. A nearly empty glass of amber liquid sat on the floor below his head.

Jeremy frowned. How long had they been gone? Two hours, give or take? Long enough for his dad to need a drink and a nap, apparently.

He didn't really remember noticing his dad drinking before the divorce. The bottles of Mason's beer had always been around, and Jeremy's mom used to pour them wine with dinner, but that had just been life, part of any normal day. Here it seemed like his dad's drinking was becoming—Jeremy didn't know what. An activity. Or something more. For the first time, watching him sleep there in the dark living room, he wondered if his dad might be keeping some secrets of his own. It was not a comfortable thought.

Jeremy made a quick bathroom stop to quietly splash his face and gargle mouthwash before heading upstairs, tiptoeing to minimize the squeaks. He set the piece of cloudy beach glass carefully on his bedside table, snatched up the bird book, and went back down.

Evan was rocking in Uncle Becker's usual chair when Jeremy reemerged with the bird book and two big glasses of water. "What took so long?" he asked.

"My dad's taking a nap. I had to sneak around so I wouldn't wake him up."

"Oh." Evan chugged his water down in one. "Well, spill it, who was right about the *feeling awful* birds?"

Jeremy flipped to the index and found the names they'd guessed. It turned out they were both wrong.

"Huh, they were American bitterns?" Evan said. "Go figure."

"I thought you were supposed to know everything about this place."

"Hey, dude, there's a lot of kinds of birds on the coast. A lot."

"Maybe you should study up, then," Jeremy said, at the same time wondering where this banter was coming from.

"Is that a challenge?"

"It could be."

Evan narrowed his eyes. "Oh, you are on." He rocked forward and got to his feet. "I gotta head back—told my grandma I'd stop by the grocery store before dinner. But I'm totally quizzing you on birds after tomorrow's run. Wait—tomorrow's Friday, right?"

"I think so."

"Okay, I'm at the shop again in the morning. We can meet same place and time as today." Evan headed down the steps. "Rest up, buddy. No puking tomorrow."

"Sure thing, Coach!" Jeremy had no idea why they'd started throwing nicknames at each other—dude? buddy? coach?—but it was amazing. "And you study." He waved the book. Evan tapped a finger to his temple and headed off, slipping into an easy lope up the beach.

Jeremy watched until he was out of sight, a fizzing blend of joy and gratitude washing over him.

He still had eleven full days to spend here in the in-between, and now he had Evan. Eleven days to go on runs and hunt for beach glass.

Eleven days to argue over seabirds. Eleven days to slip between the cracks, like Evan had said, and build a whole new story just between him and his new friend.

Jeremy stood, poised on his steps at the edge of the world, looking out at the sun on the ocean, dreaming big, windy dreams.

Nine

FRIDAY, JUNE 29

The Heermann's gull was floating just above the house, its wings holding a hard curve against the wind while one glittering eye fixed on Jeremy. He stood on the roof eyeing it back, a hand raised to block the sun, wondering how it would feel to be held up by the wind like that: calm, steady, trusting in its support. Down on the beach, a little kid screamed with laughter, making a dog bark, and between one blink and the next, the gull leaned sideways into the air and disappeared.

Jeremy let out a breath and stooped back to his work. The gutters weren't going to clean themselves.

The morning had started like the others before it, with Jeremy fending for himself while his dad filled the living space with paperwork. Jeremy ate his toast and cereal on the porch, trying to decide how he felt about the taste of Froot Loops combined with the smell of the ocean.

"Jer." His dad was hammering away at the laptop when Jeremy

brought his dishes back inside. "I want you to start with the gutters."

"What?"

"The gutters. You've had enough of a break to mess around; chores start today. I talked to your uncle, and he wants those done first. Once they're clear, you can scrub the roof clean and hose it down after."

"Oh."

His dad gave the keyboard a climactic stab and sat up, looking over. "I saw a ladder behind the house and some buckets. You're not scared of heights, right?"

Jeremy shook his head, though he honestly wasn't sure.

"Great," said his dad. "Finish the roof this morning, and you can have the afternoon to do whatever you want."

Just like that, Jeremy had found himself tugging at the ladder behind the beach house, ripping it free from the climbing vine that had coiled around its rungs, thinking how this was just one more thing he could never tell his mom. She would be furious at the idea of him being sent up a ladder with no supervision, no lecture, and no safety gear. Knowing her, she would have insisted on a crash helmet.

He found a pair of work gloves, at least, stashed between two of the buckets buried under weeds beside the ladder. On instinct he shook one, and when a large brown spider and an earwig fell out, he turned both gloves inside out and whacked them against the wall for a full minute before pulling them on. They were at least two sizes too big, but they were better than nothing.

The ladder was metal, wide-legged and sturdy, and light enough for Jeremy to lift on his own. He carried it around to the north wall of the house by the garbage and recycling bins, settling it with a *thunk* against the sagging plastic gutters. Its rungs squeaked as he gave it a test shake, then started up, a bucket dangling from one hand.

Up close, the roof was a mess. Gull poop streaked the sides and completely blanketed the thin plastic ridgeline running along the very top. The gutters were overflowing with pine needles, which must have been there long enough to start breaking down because tiny seedlings were growing out here and there, battling the wind and reaching for the sun. Jeremy hung his bucket from a latch on the ladder and got to work, feeling slightly bad as he scraped up the baby trees. He scraped up plenty more earwigs, too, plus spiders, centipedes, dead wasps, and even—somehow—an earthworm. No wonder Uncle Becker wanted the gutters done first.

He scraped and dug with his gloved hands as far as he could safely reach on one side, then the other, then stopped, realizing exactly what he was up against. He would have to climb down, empty the bucket, move the ladder a few feet, and climb back up, over and over and over, on both sides of the house. His legs were already sore from yesterday; going up and down so much would definitely wipe him out, and that would ruin his afternoon run with Evan, right when he was determined to make a better impression.

What if instead he climbed up onto the roof and worked his way along the edge, emptying the gutters straight onto the ground? He could be done in half the time, with way less stress on his knees. The ground was already scattered with pine needles and stuff anyway. All he'd have to do was sweep up after.

A bit surprised at his own daring, Jeremy climbed the last few steps of the ladder and eased himself forward onto the tiles. He found his balance against the slope and stood all the way up, relieved to discover that, no, he didn't have a problem with heights. He gazed down at the beach and out to the Pacific. The view was the same as his bedroom window just a few feet below, but the world looked totally different from up here: bigger, with the horizon somehow farther away.

That was when the gull appeared, floating on the wind, its head cocking side to side so one beady eye at a time could examine him. Given the state of the gutters, this particular gull had probably never seen a person up there before. They watched each other, and then the dog barked, the gull disappeared, and Jeremy bent to get on with his task.

He was distracted almost immediately, however, this time by the crunch of tires pulling into the driveway.

Jeremy ignored it at first, figuring it was Uncle Becker coming to pal around with his dad like always. The engine stopped, and he heard a car door open and slam. Then another car door open and slam. And another. And another.

Jeremy looked around. Had Becker brought friends?

He stood up, one hand out in case he slipped, and edged across the roof to see.

A strange blue car sat in the driveway behind his dad's. It had four surfboards—two big, two small—strapped to its top. It was definitely not Uncle Becker.

Jeremy scrambled higher, ignoring the fresh gull poop smearing on his work gloves, and made it to the peak in time to see a whole family walking from the driveway toward the house. They were white, blond, and smiling: a mom with a ponytail, a dad with a military buzz cut, two daughters maybe a year or two younger than Jeremy. They reached the porch and disappeared from view.

He heard someone knock on the door.

"Hello? Mr. Ryden?" said a woman's voice.

There was a pause, then the sound of the door opening.

"Ah, hello!" the woman said. "We're the Lewises. We saw your car, though we didn't expect you'd be here. Is the house all ready?"

"What?" That was Jeremy's dad.

"The house. Is it ready? I know we're a tiny bit early."

Jeremy inched up higher on his perch. He could imagine his father's expression, taking in the smiling family, looking from them to their car and back.

"Early for what?" Jeremy's dad was speaking a shade louder than usual. "Why are you people here?"

"Well, we're staying here, Mr. Ryden." The woman gave a laugh. "We confirmed the reservation with you."

"Confirmed the— Oh! You mean my brother."

"I'm sorry?"

"My brother, Becker Ryden. He owns this place." Another pause. "Were you those people who were gonna stay here? He said you canceled."

"*Those people?*" said the man.

"No! No, that's incorrect." The woman was making a point of keeping her voice bright and friendly. "We *thought* we'd have to cancel at first, but we worked it out and wrote the same day to ask if we could simply start four days later. We have a hold on this property through the tenth of July. Your brother confirmed."

"Couldn't have. *I'm* staying here until the tenth. Me and my boy. Becker knows that."

A face appeared in Jeremy's view: the younger of the two girls, stepping back to take in the house.

"Who's that?" she asked, pointing at him and interrupting the grown-ups. There was a shuffling, and the whole group appeared down on the dirt and sand, necks craned to look up at Jeremy. The woman—Ms. Lewis, he supposed—had her mouth pressed together in a hard line. Her husband just looked confused.

"That's Jeremy, my son. Come on down, Jer. There's . . . company."

Jeremy missed what the group said next as he scrabbled across the scratchy roofing to the ladder. Getting back on was trickier than he'd expected. His descent started off okay once he'd managed it, but just before the ground, his right glove snagged on a rung and his hand slipped out, swinging free. He dropped the bucket, lost his balance grabbing for it, and tumbled the last few feet right into the nearby recycling bin. Cans and beer bottles crashed out everywhere.

"I'm fine!" Jeremy yelled, out of pure instinct. "Everything's fine!"

He got to his feet, checking for damage, then stopped, staring at the avalanche of bottles. He counted back, thinking. Yes, it had only been four days since they'd arrived. How had his dad gotten through all this? Even with Uncle Becker's help? And *when*? Sure, there had usually been a bottle sitting beside the laptop while his dad worked, but Jeremy had never wondered about how quickly they were being replaced.

The certainty that his father was covering something up settled into Jeremy's mind like pine needles filling a gutter. At the exact same moment, he realized he didn't want the other family to come investigating and see this. He didn't want his father exposed. He abandoned the mess and darted around the corner of the house, ready to make up some story if anyone asked about the crash.

His arrival didn't even get a glance. His dad was still talking, but so was Ms. Lewis, pulling papers from her bag in the process.

"No, no! I'm sorry, but I promise you," she said, "I have the printed email right here, and look. Look!" She pushed the papers forward.

"Seriously?" Jeremy's father said, taking them. "You printed your email booking?"

Jeremy was surprised his dad was surprised. It was exactly what his mom had always done. *Cell phones can fail*, she used to say. *Computers can die. Networks can go out. It's never a bad idea to bring confirmation you can hold in your hand and point to.* Had his dad really never noticed?

The thought of his mom raised a sudden, awful fear in Jeremy's mind. What if the Lewises turned out to be right? What if they had a real claim on the place, and Uncle Becker would have to follow some state law or other, and he and his dad would have to leave? His mom would be furious when they showed up back at the house a whole week and a half early, cutting into the privacy of her packing time. And what about Evan? They were supposed to go running in a few hours! Their friendship had only just gotten started!

They couldn't leave. Not now, not like this. They just couldn't.

"Whatever," Jeremy's father said, barely glancing at the papers before shoving them back at Ms. Lewis. "I don't care what that says. Me and Jer are here, and we're staying."

"We have the booking." Ms. Lewis's arms were crossed.

"Great! Then let's ask Becker!" Jeremy's dad pulled out his phone and stabbed at it. The Lewis grown-ups tilted their heads together in a whispered huddle.

The girls had backed away from the house toward the sand, keeping their distance as they looked out at the beach. If Jeremy's mom had been there, she would have asked him to take them on a walk down to the waves, removing all three kids from the awkward grown-up dance going on. But his dad was the parent out here.

"Becker! Hey!" Jeremy's dad barked into his phone. "Listen, there's some family here. The Lowells or something—"

"The Lewises!"

"The Lewises. Yeah, those ones . . . Well, *they* think they are! And they've got these emails . . . I know . . . I know . . . I know! Don't yell at me! Look—here, you talk to her!"

Jeremy's father thrust out his phone like an Olympic torch, and Ms. Lewis stepped forward to take it.

"Hello, Mr. Ryden," she said, almost managing her friendly, patient tone again. "Yes . . . Yes . . . Yes, we did, but then we wrote you back, you remember? I have the email in front of me . . . Printed, yes . . . Well, it does clearly show your reply of *All good, thanks for letting me know* occurring after our second email rescheduling ... What? ... How were we to know you hadn't seen it? I mean, we were a little confused when our deposit was returned, but we thought that was simply because we'd be staying fewer days and you'd sort it out later."

She looked to her husband and shook her head, her eyes going wide and furious. Her free hand was clenched at her side, veins standing up on the back.

Jeremy looked to his father; he was staring at the log marking the end of the driveway, his arms crossed and his face set.

Ms. Lewis kept up her argument with Becker, interrupting and protesting, until at last she shouted, "All right! Fine! But you are making a *huge* mistake!" She lowered the phone and turned to her husband. "Looks like we're not staying here after all."

"Told you," Jeremy's dad said, coming back to life with a smile.

Ms. Lewis handed over the phone, glaring. "Well, I promise that your brother will regret this," she said. "I will be writing a *very* decisive review of his business and its practices and sharing it with everyone I know!"

His dad laughed, but Jeremy gnawed his lip, feeling guilty. She had a point. The mix-up had just ruined the Lewises' vacation. Who knew, maybe they really needed it.

"And for what it's worth," Ms. Lewis went on, not bothering to hide her anger as she waved her daughters back into the car, "it seems a real waste for this house to be going to, you know, *two people* over the Fourth of July when it could be going to an entire *family!*"

"Hey!" Jeremy's dad stepped forward. "This is a *family*, too, and we have just as much—"

"I'm just saying!" the woman yelled, getting behind the wheel, her silent husband shaking his head beside her.

"Well, *I'm* saying—"

Two slamming car doors cut him off, and the Lewises backed out of the driveway, their tires spitting dust and gravel as they zoomed out of sight.

Ms. Lewis's parting shot filled the prickling silence that followed, dismissing Jeremy and his dad's right to the house, dismissing them as a family. Jeremy waited to see how his dad would react. It was strange, but to him, it felt like the first real thing the two of them had shared since getting there.

His dad ran a hand through his hair, squeezed the back of his neck, then blew out his cheeks. "All right, show's over," he said. "Back to work. This ain't no vacation." He turned and went into the house, leaving the door hanging wide. Jeremy heard the refrigerator open and close.

Wondering exactly who his dad had been talking to, Jeremy went to clean up the bottles.

Ten

SATURDAY, JUNE 30

Late morning the following day, Jeremy found himself squinting down into the depths of a teeming tide pool, his eyes watering from the sun shimmer flashing on the surface. Evan crouched beside him, balancing easily on the barnacle-covered rocks, pointing out the orange sea stars, spiny urchins, and purple anemones going about their business in the water.

The summer weekend was in full swing on the coast, and the two boys were taking a long, wandering break in the middle of their third run.

Their second run the day before had gone well. After his morning of gutter cleaning and roof scrubbing, not to mention the encounter with the Lewises, Jeremy had been more than ready to leave the beach house behind and head out with Evan. He'd even managed to ignore his stinging blisters and aching lungs. Best of all, he'd managed the whole run—all the way out and back—without throwing up once.

He'd felt downright proud, even though he knew his improvement was almost entirely thanks to Evan, who'd kept their pace close to a jog without being asked and invented excuses to stop if he saw Jeremy was struggling. The excuses were mostly things like washed-up jellyfish or extra-big crab shells, but sometimes Evan would point out a bird and start a friendly argument about it until Jeremy had his breath back. It was an obvious tactic, but Jeremy appreciated it.

They'd each checked their copies of the bird book again when they got home, and by dinnertime had added *sanderling* (happy), *Caspian tern* (high five), and *great blue heron* (hungry) to their bird code list. Jeremy appointed himself secretary and started keeping track on a folded piece of paper he'd been using as a bookmark.

So, it had been an easy yes when Evan suggested an early run that morning, heading north for a change so Jeremy could get a look at the driftwood forts.

The forts had turned out to be occupied already by big, noisy groups, but Jeremy got a decent view of most of the lopsided wooden structures as they jogged past. They'd run steadily after that, keeping up a good pace until Evan called a stop to check out the sights, and Jeremy, panting and sweating hard, responded with two enthusiastic thumbs-up.

"Come on," said Evan, bopping Jeremy on the forearm and hopping to his feet. "One tide pool down. We gotta see what's in all the others!"

Jeremy, thrilled and a little light-headed from the casual touch, followed.

They worked their way up and down the long spur of sandstone that housed the pools, trading places with families and kids as they explored the dozens of minute ecosystems revealed by the tide. Jeremy felt almost like a kid himself when Evan, laughing, found one with a hermit crab in it, roaming through the seaweed with a plastic doll's head on its back as a home.

The stretch of beach where they'd chosen to rest was busy—partly because of the tide pools, and partly because of the nearby parking lot that connected directly to the coastal highway. It was a perfect lure for families and road-tripping tourists, and the crowds had shown up in force. Jeremy even spotted a combination ice cream and hot dog stand setting up nearby, already attracting a line.

When they'd had their fill of tide pools, Jeremy and Evan found a decent sitting spot on a nearby shelf of rock, crusted with blue-black mussels below and curving above to form a backrest. They sat comfortably, not speaking, kicking their legs and watching the sunbathing people and excited dogs and a scattering of dark, long-necked birds diving over and over again into the sea.

Jeremy felt himself filling up with a warm, grateful happiness as he sat there. The first run with Evan had felt like a miracle, and the second like a dream. Now he was starting to let himself believe that this was all really happening. He and Evan had hung out three times now, and as far as he could tell, Evan seemed fine with keeping it going.

It looked like he and Runner Boy were truly becoming friends.

It was Evan who finally broke their silence, and when he did, he took Jeremy completely by surprise.

"Hey, would you ever want to be a bird?"

Jeremy heaved his mind back to the real world and the Evan beside him. "Sorry? A what?"

"I think it would be fun. Look at those western gulls." Evan pointed to a cluster of large gray-and-white birds with yellow beaks pecking in the surf. A handful more bobbed on the waves beyond. "They are western gulls, agreed?"

Jeremy, still trying to catch up, peered at them. "Agreed."

"Well, think about their lives. They get to walk around on land, fly in the air, *and* paddle on the water. That's a pretty cool combination of skills for one animal."

"Huh," said Jeremy. He nodded. "You're right. And I guess most birds never have to worry about falling or heights or anything, since they can just put out their wings."

"Exactly! I think seagulls have it best, though, since when they get tired, they can just look down at the water and go, 'Oh, hey, a chair!'"

Jeremy laughed. Out on the beach, a French bulldog got too close to the gulls, and they lifted into the air, complaining. Most settled back on the safety of the water, but three of them kept climbing, rising into the sky, riding the currents of the onshore wind. Evan and Jeremy tilted their necks to watch.

"That would be the greatest part," said Evan. "Just soaring like that, taking in the view, screaming if you felt like it."

"I wonder if they get that roller-coaster feeling in their stomachs when they go up or down too fast," Jeremy said. "Like, look!" One of the gulls curved into a dive, flashing back in a steep arc to the waves. "That was a sixty-foot drop at least! That has to feel weird. Plus, do their ears pop? Does the wind make their tiny eyes water?"

From the corner of his eye, he saw Evan glance over at him, his mouth forming one of his beautiful smiles.

"And what about different weather?" Jeremy continued. He was talking too much now, but he couldn't help it. He wanted Evan to keep looking at him that way. "They fly in the rain sometimes, right? That's got to feel weird. Imagine rain tapping on your open wings. Or flying in snow and getting ice crystals up your beak. Or how really hot sun must feel when it's shining thorough your feathers."

It was Evan's turn to laugh. "Okay, wow, you've thought about this way more than I have," he said. "You *definitely* want to be a bird."

Jeremy felt his face go warm and kept it pointed at the sky. "I wouldn't mind," he murmured, watching the gulls glide, proud and free, through the high, churning air.

"Hello, boys!" a voice called suddenly. "How you doing, Evan? And it's Jeremy, right?"

Jeremy brought his eyes down to earth to find Sandy from the Grill standing nearby, her hands on her hips. He instantly scooted away from Evan, making certain there was a normal, friendly amount of space between them.

The last time Jeremy had seen Sandy she'd been in her work clothes. Today she was wearing a fitted teal sundress with cap sleeves and a navy-blue bucket hat. The ends of her blond hair curled around her face in the wind. Jeremy thought she really was very pretty.

"Hey, Sandy," said Evan, who clearly already knew her. "We're fine. How are you doing?"

"Well, it's my morning off, it's a beautiful day, and I'm hanging out at the beach, so pretty great! What are you boys up to?" Sandy craned her neck to the sky where Jeremy had been looking. "Bird-watching?"

Evan nodded. "We came up here on a run, I showed Jeremy the tide pools, and now this."

Sandy beamed. "I'm so happy you two found each other," she said. "Summer is always more fun with people your own age. It wouldn't be the same hanging around with your dad and uncle all the time, would it, Jeremy? Even though sometimes your uncle does act like a kid!" She winked at him. Jeremy didn't know what to do with that. "And, Evan, this is your first year without any of your other cousins here, isn't it?"

"Second," Evan said.

"Oh, of course! I'm sure you're extra glad Jeremy showed up to be some company for you this time, then!"

Evan agreed that he was glad, but Jeremy ducked his head, fiddling with a barnacle on the rock. Sandy was being nice, but she was also super close to making things uncomfortable. Some grown-ups never really got that they didn't always have to comment. Not everything needed to be pointed to and talked about.

"So, what is it about the birds?" Sandy asked. "Are the seagulls around here, like, super cool?"

"Nah," said Evan, hiding a smile. "I mean, kind of. We were just talking about what it would be like to be one."

"Oh! Well!" Sandy scanned the beach. "In that case, I want to be one of those, if we're choosing." She pointed to the long-necked diving birds Jeremy had spotted earlier. "They're cormorants; I forget what kind. I know they look sort of plain from here, but if the sun hits them, you can see that they're actually iridescent—blue and purple and green and everything." She held a hand over her eyes and watched a pair of the birds rise, then drop into the sea, folding their wings at the last second and barely making a splash. "I just think cormorants are so beautiful."

Jeremy and Evan turned to each other.

"Cormorant?" Evan said.

"Beautiful?" said Jeremy.

They gave a nod in unison, smiling.

Jeremy could have cheered; they had another word for their seabird code! And what a perfect word. He almost blushed again, imagining how he wanted to use it. The idea of telling Evan he was *cormorant* made his insides dive as dramatically as the bird itself.

"Okay, then!" Sandy turned back to them, and Jeremy was grateful she had missed their exchange. "Thanks for the food for thought, boys! I should run, but it was awesome seeing you both. I hope you come by the Grill again sometime, Jeremy! And bring your father!"

They all waved and said goodbye, and Sandy continued on down the beach.

"She seems nice," Jeremy said.

"She is," said Evan. "She kind of reminds me of my fourth-grade teacher sometimes, but yeah, mostly she's great." He turned to Jeremy. "Hey, are you getting *great blue heron*?"

Jeremy had to think for a moment, then smiled wide. "I could eat."

"Same. Did you bring money this time like I said?"

Evan had mentioned the possibility of weekend beach vendors in his texts that morning, and Jeremy had taken his advice and brought ten dollars safely sealed inside a sandwich bag.

"Yup!"

"Nice. Let's get food first, then walk back. I think we've done enough running for today."

They hopped off their rock, and Evan led the way over to the ice-cream-and-hot-dog stand, where they joined the line.

"Do you know Sandy just from coming here in the summers?" Jeremy asked.

Evan nodded. "She and my grandma are friends. They started a Rosemont small-business-owners club a few years back. A couple of my cousins did summer jobs at the Grill, too." His eyes went wide, and he snapped his fingers, pointing at Jeremy. "Dang, speaking of my cousins, I totally meant to tell you! There's this fishing trip my uncle takes us all on every summer, total family tradition. They're driving down to get me tomorrow."

"Oh!" Jeremy's good mood cracked down the middle. "How long is the trip?"

Evan shrugged. "Three days, usually. It depends on whether we hit our catch quota or not. And how well we're all getting along."

"Oh," Jeremy said again as the line shifted forward. It was all he could think to say. Three days without Evan? Without runs? Without hanging out? What was he going to do with himself? Okay, he'd planned on spending most of his time alone here back when they'd arrived, but that had been before Evan. Before the seabird language. Before . . . everything.

"It's usually pretty fun," Evan went on. "Though my cousins are all teenagers now, and some of them can get a bit obnoxious. Still." He turned to Jeremy. "Do you, um, wanna come along?"

Jeremy stared at him, his face blank. "What?"

"Do you want to come with?" Evan met Jeremy's eyes, then looked away. "It'd be totally fine. My cousins bring friends sometimes. Unless you think your dad won't let you?"

Jeremy was having trouble staying on his feet.

Evan had just asked him to join his family fishing trip. After only knowing Jeremy four days.

But even as part of him thrilled at the unbelievable proof of friendship, a louder voice inside him was busy sounding alarms. He had to be careful around Evan as it was, keeping his feelings and reactions in check. Spending three entire days together would make that harder, and there would be new dangers, too: the uncle and all those teenage cousins. That was too many eyes and way too many unknowns.

The more Jeremy pictured it, the more he knew it was impossible.

"No," he said after what felt like an hour of standing there with his mouth open. "No, I don't think my dad would let me." He didn't think that, actually, but his dad was the perfect excuse. "I'm sorry. And thank you! Thank you so much. That's super nice of you. Just, my dad . . . he's weird about stuff like this."

Evan's face fell, but he didn't press.

"I get it," he said. "No worries." They moved forward another place in line.

They remained silent through the rest of their wait. Jeremy felt awful about lying to Evan, but he knew going on a spur-of-the-moment trip with a bunch of strangers just wasn't an option for him. That sort of thing was for confident people who weren't busy keeping pieces of themselves hidden. People like his uncle Becker. People like Evan.

The looming separation weighed on Jeremy all the rest of the day, but he did his best to shove it out of his mind as they ate their hot-dog-and-ice-cream lunch and wandered back toward town. For now, he and Evan were still together, still talking and joking and hanging out, and until that changed, he wanted to savor every last passing, golden second.

Eleven

SUNDAY, JULY 1

Jeremy woke up late on Sunday morning, his sixth morning on the coast. He stretched, smiling at the satisfying ache in his legs, and peered out the window at a milky-blue sky shot with long ruffles of clouds. Plovers and black-legged kittiwakes were flocking along the beach. He could smell coffee from downstairs.

He turned to check his phone, filling with happiness at the sight of a text from Evan.

Hey! Forgot to say yesterday but we're heading out early. As in now. Bye!

Jeremy stared at the screen, his happiness spiraling away. The text had been sent an hour ago. Evan was already gone.

Hey, he texted back, then stopped.

What should he say? He was already missing Evan, but he should be excited for his friend, right? Or at least pretend to be?

> Awesome! Have fun! Catch some sharks for me!

Oh, no no-no-no-no, he did not just hit send!

> I mean, NOT sharks, because they're protected or endangered I think? But catch a good fish. Lots of good fish. If you want to.

> Sorry, I just woke up.

He was still staring in horror when the first reply came back.

> Haha, lazy. Was up hours ago

> Already almost there. I promise not to catch sharks

> You gonna run on your own?

The simple question sent Jeremy's foggy morning brain spinning. Run? On his own? What would be the point? He only ran to hang out with Evan. Anyway, running solo would make him super visible. What if people stared at him? What if they noticed how often he had to stop? Or how red he got? Or how much sweat monsooned down his face? He could think of a thousand reasons to say no right off the top of his head.

But Evan was probably expecting him to say yes. He'd probably be disappointed if Jeremy didn't run on his own. He'd probably think things over on this awesome fishing trip with his cousins and decide he didn't want to be friends after all.

Jeremy attempted a nonanswer.

> Haha, will see. Have to get up and start the day first.

Lazy

Jeremy smiled.

> Have fun today!

You too

The world outside the window hadn't actually changed in the last five minutes, but it didn't seem nearly so bright and sunny as Jeremy pulled on jeans and a T-shirt and made his way downstairs.

His dad and Uncle Becker were talking in the kitchen. Jeremy waved, mumbling a greeting as he ducked into the bathroom. When he emerged, his dad was settling in at the table and Becker was filling a travel mug from the coffeepot. The porch door stood open, letting in a cool breeze off the beach and the morning screams of the birds.

"We were just talking about you, Jeremy," his dad said. "I'm going to be putting in some serious time on these course proposals so I can relax over the Fourth, so I'll need this place to be quiet."

Jeremy filled the toaster and pressed the down button, wondering when he'd ever made enough noise to distract his father from his work. He nodded. "Can do."

"I know," said his dad. "Because you're going up to Klatsand with your uncle today."

Jeremy's gaze snapped to Becker, who raised his mug and smiled. "I'm looking at a place I might buy for a rental. Thought you'd want to get away from your old man, see a bit of the coast. And I could use another pair of eyes on the house."

The toast popped up. The bread was barely warm, but Jeremy pulled it out and began buttering, his back to the grown-ups.

"Jeremy?" his dad said. "This is where you thank your uncle for inviting you."

A minor battle was going on inside Jeremy. He'd already been feeling bruised about Evan taking off, and now his father's erratic, heavy-handed parenting was seriously getting to him. He wondered what would happen if he just refused to go.

But the urge died as the second half of his battling brain pointed out that a trip up the coast was kind of a perfect distraction. It would be better than wandering the beach on his own all day, anyway. Or lying around in his room counting down the minutes until Evan came back. It might even give him some stories to share.

"Thanks, Uncle Becker," he said, turning around. "That sounds great."

"All right!" Becker saluted with his coffee mug. "It's a ninety-minute drive each way, so heave yourself together and let's hit the road."

Twenty minutes later, Becker was pulling his truck out of the driveway, Jeremy in the passenger seat beside him. Jeremy's father had practically thrown them out of the house, repeating how much work he had to do, and Jeremy had been left thinking again about the contrast between his parents. In his mom's world, this would have counted as a full day trip, which would have meant going over the route ahead of time, packing plenty of snacks, preselecting a place to stop for lunch, double-checking to be sure all cell phones were charged, and making sure everyone had emergency money for pay phones or bus fare just in case.

His dad had done exactly none of that, but Jeremy had enough of his mom's voice permanently lodged between his ears to have thrown together his own bag of supplies. The backpack resting between his feet held sunscreen, a bottle of water, three granola bars, flip-flops, a beach towel, and the bird book. He also had what was left of his money, and Becker turned out to have a car adapter, so there were no worries about charging his phone.

Becker had the radio on before they were out of the driveway, familiar classic rock twanging through the buzzy speakers, and despite the disappointment and resentment of the morning, Jeremy felt a curl of anticipation as they made their way toward town. If nothing else, this would be something different.

They made one final stop for gas, and Becker ran inside the mini-mart. When he climbed back behind the wheel, a crinkly plastic bag landed in Jeremy's lap.

"What's this?" Jeremy asked.

"Road trip fuel." Becker stashed an identical bag in the cup holder beside the parking brake. He looked over, seeing Jeremy's expression. "What?"

"Gummy orange slices?"

"The only road trip fuel! Hasn't your dad ever taught you that?"

Jeremy shook his head.

Becker made a big show of looking shocked, but he was smiling. "It's family tradition! Your dad and I have been eating these on road trips since we were younger than you are. Dig in and catch up, little man."

"Um, thanks." Jeremy tucked the bag into the storage space on the door. "But are we— I mean, does this even count as a road trip? We're only gonna be gone for, like, half a day."

"Don't fight the driver, Jer," said Becker good-naturedly. "If I say my nephew and I are going on a road trip, my nephew and I are going on a road trip."

He fired the engine to life, cranked the radio up, and started singing at the top of his lungs as they slipped onto the winding coastal road.

A minute or two later, Jeremy realized he was humming along.

Twelve

It didn't take long on the road for Jeremy to realize he'd really needed something like this trip. He'd been nervous at first about spending so much time with Becker, since his uncle liked to tease and joke and poke at people's feelings sometimes, but he was pleasantly surprised. Becker left him to himself, and the music joined with the world passing by to create an easy silence between them. Jeremy still felt the ache of his separation from Evan, but as the miles sped by, the rest of the morning's heaviness eased and faded and finally vanished.

Their road wove through small towns and suburbs and curved past fields and farms. There were sheep in some of the fields, horses in others, and once Jeremy got a glimpse of what might have been alpacas, their long, fuzzy necks all turning to follow the truck. Every now and then the view on their left opened up, and they could see the white-edged waves of the Pacific, and the sand and craggy arms of rock basking in the sun.

The same sun slanted in through Jeremy's window most of

the way, hot on his forearm and the fabric of his jeans. He stared out at the passing world, listening to Becker murmur along to the radio, letting himself relax into the warmth and the drone of the engine.

"Hey, dreamer boy, wakey-wakey. We're almost there."

Jeremy looked around, realizing he'd been half-asleep. He sat up, stretching a cramp from his neck.

"You doing okay? Need water or a bathroom break or anything?" Becker asked. Jeremy shook his head.

"I thought we'd check out the house first, then go get lunch. Sound good?"

"Great." Jeremy was surprised again. Those were parent questions, the kind his mom would have asked. Apparently, Uncle Becker could be pretty different when his big brother wasn't around.

A few more turns took them into Klatsand, a coastal town roughly the same size as Rosemont, though a lot less touristy. Becker pulled over beside a wooden fence tangled with morning glory to check the map on his phone.

"We're looking for a lime-green house," he said, pulling back onto the road. "Two stories, big deck. Keep your eyes peeled."

They spotted it at the same time, although it would have been pretty hard to miss. The house sat on a small bluff, the last in a row of cookie-cutter homes, and it certainly was green. Not actual lime green, but a fluorescent, tropical-cruise imitation of the color. A deck of golden wood extended from the west side onto a scraggly lawn, where patchy grass changed to rock as it neared the edge of the bluff and what had to be an epic view of the horizon.

They parked behind a Range Rover in the driveway and got out. Becker rang the doorbell, then knocked, and a short woman wearing cream slacks and a purple blouse answered, introducing herself as Carol, the realtor. Everyone shook hands, and Carol invited them to look around the house and let her know if they had any questions.

Jeremy braced himself, preparing for Becker to drag him into a loud, jokey trip around the place, pointing out good spots for climbing into bedroom windows or making out with girls. But his uncle just called out, "Let me know what you think, Jer," and disappeared up the stairs, taking pictures with his phone. Carol retreated to her laptop at the kitchen counter, and Jeremy, surprised, found himself free to explore however he liked.

The house was being shown empty—no staged furniture, no knickknacks, no pictures on the walls—so walking around wasn't as weird as it could have been. Jeremy wandered, the thick dove-gray carpeting soft under his feet, trying to figure out why each room he went into was painted a slightly different shade of pastel blue. Compared with the bright and almost deliberately tacky outside, the cool tones made the inside seem sort of dull and flat.

He walked down the hall, hearing Becker on the floor above, and passed doors opening onto a den with a fireplace, a half bathroom, a utility room for the washer and dryer. All of them felt off, somehow—too big, or too small, or too narrow. The half bathroom had a weird nook tucked into one corner, a head-high recess as wide and deep as a microwave. Jeremy couldn't imagine what it was for. It made the room feel uncomfortable.

He wondered what sort of house his mom had picked out in Beaverton, and whether he would like it. It was strange to think whatever place she'd settled on might be his new home, if he decided to go that way. His home for his teenage years, and eventually high school. His home in a new city, where so much about his life would probably change. He hoped at the very least he would like the view from his bedroom window. He could probably trust his mom to pick something decent, but this place was making him aware that the safe, familiar house in Corvallis was a real point in his dad's favor.

He headed back up the hall, getting a view of how squished the front door was against the wall of the dining room. Why would the architects put it there? The window beside it was strangely low, too, so you'd have to be sitting down to get any kind of view of outside. *It's like nothing here really fits together,* he thought. *Nothing connects with anything else.* Carol, tapping at her computer, gave him a quick smile as he cut through the dining room, and he returned it awkwardly, heading for the deck. He'd seen enough.

Outside, the sea wind slammed into him, and he instantly felt better. He closed the sliding door and crossed the golden wood, the sun on his shoulders, the air full of salt and the oily smell of fresh varnish.

He stepped down to the lawn and kept going, heading right up to the gravel and rocks on the edge of the bluff. The Pacific Ocean stretched out before him, cormorants wheeling above it. He put his hands in his pockets and stared out for a long time.

It was a beautiful spot. He definitely wouldn't mind staying somewhere with a front yard like this. But the inside of the house . . . that was all wrong.

Jeremy was struck by a new appreciation for the beach house and his own gabled attic room. That had been an easy fit, comfortable from the second he walked in. It was strange how houses could be so different, how the same person could fit or not depending on where they were.

Picturing the beach house made him think of his running shoes sitting at the foot of his bed, and that made him think of Evan. Evan was somewhere out there right now, riding in a boat with all his cousins and the deep ocean beneath them. Did Evan feel trapped out there? Was he having fun? Was he missing running?

Was he missing Jeremy?

He heard the screen door open and close behind him, then shoes thudding on the deck.

"Well, what do you think?" Becker called cheerfully, striding across the grass. "Obviously, it's a lot bigger than what I normally rent out. It'd be a major purchase, and I'd have to work to keep it filled. But I could charge more, get in some groups, not just small family trips. Could mean a lot of money."

Jeremy reeled in his thoughts with an effort. "I don't think you should," he said, surprising himself with the certainty in his voice. Becker came to a stop beside him, eyebrows raised.

"Why not? It's got a stellar view."

"Sure. But the house just feels, you know . . . off. Like parts of it aren't where they should be. Like it doesn't know what it is. Or what it wants to be."

"Huh." Becker looked back at the house, crossing his arms. "You know what? I think you're right. I got kind of a strange vibe myself. The closets upstairs are all the weirdest design, weird pocket rooms, like cells. And there's almost too much house, you know? Like the architects were trying to show off but didn't know how."

For the fourth time that day, Jeremy was surprised by his uncle.

"Yeah," he said. "Exactly."

"Lucky I had you here to point it out, or I might have gotten stuck with a house I couldn't rent!" Becker slapped Jeremy on the back. "So, let's jet. I've got to check out with that Carol lady, but wanna meet me at the truck in two minutes? We can go find a spot for lunch."

They ate at a chain seafood restaurant another town up. Over their fish and chips, Becker told Jeremy in exact detail all the things he'd need to know if he ever wanted to buy a house himself someday. Jeremy hadn't asked, but it kept him from having to think up things to say during the meal, and by the end, he'd actually learned a lot. It turned out Becker had been self-employed since dropping out of college and had racked up plenty of useful knowledge he was more than happy to share.

When their bored teenage server dropped off the check, Jeremy pulled out his wallet, but Becker shooed him down. "Oh, no, no, no, no, no," he said, snatching up the slip of paper. "You're not that grown-up yet, buddy. Where'd you get money from, anyway?"

Jeremy winced, then realized he was probably safe telling Becker. "My mom gave me some. Before we left."

His uncle nodded. "Sounds like Beth. Don't worry." He raised a hand at the look on Jeremy's face. "I won't tell your dad. But you're still not paying for food. Get yourself a job first; then we can talk about splitting the check."

"My friend Evan has a job. He works for his grandma at her shop in Rosemont."

Jeremy did not know what made him say it. He hadn't even been thinking about Evan just then.

Fear shimmered back into his afternoon.

"Oh yeah?" Becker folded the check around a credit card and set it on the edge of the table. "Well, be careful who you tell that to, Jer. Even for a family business, a kid your age isn't really allowed to work."

Jeremy's fear started spiraling. He hadn't considered that. "He just helps out behind the counter. He's really good at talking with customers and stuff. I've seen him."

"That's nice, but it doesn't change anything. Does his grandma pay him?"

"I think she adds it into his allowance?"

"Ha! Well, okay. That's still just on the wrong side of technically legal, though." He dropped his voice to a dramatic whisper. "So, keep it under wraps."

"You won't tell anyone, will you?" Jeremy said, fighting down a bubble of panic. "About Evan?" Why on earth had he told Uncle Becker anything?

"Not a soul. Any friend of my one and only nephew is a friend of mine. This Evan kid is practically family."

Still off balance, Jeremy felt himself smile. It was a big smile, a dead giveaway of every feeling he was trying to keep hidden, but luckily

Becker was busy flagging down their server to come pick up the check, and he didn't notice a thing.

"Cool, cool, cool," Becker said as they pulled on their seat belts in the truck. "We've done some driving, we looked at a house we didn't want, and we ate fried food. So, what's next? It's only two o'clock; we've got time for adventuring. Or would you rather head home?"

Jeremy considered. Heading home would mean going back to the town, the beach, the house. All the places where Evan wasn't.

"Let's keep going," he answered. "Is there anything to do around here?"

A stop at another gas station got them directions to a famous local rock formation, and on the way there, a road sign sent them detouring to a historic working lighthouse.

The lighthouse was closed to visitors, but they walked around outside, checking out the view with the other tourists. A family of five—two moms and three rowdy sons—asked Becker to take their photo. It took a while to find a spot where he could fit them and the lighthouse in the shot, and in the end the whole family had to squint full into the afternoon sun, but they didn't seem to mind. Jeremy watched them walk away, all chatting happily, and wondered how that kind of life would feel. Parents content together. Multiple siblings. A constant wall of people to lean against and learn from. There wouldn't be much privacy for keeping your secrets safe, but maybe that wouldn't matter so much.

The famous rock formation turned out to be about as exciting as a peanut butter sandwich, but there was a bird sanctuary attached to it, and Jeremy had a nice time wandering around reading all the informational signs under their protective plastic covers. It felt good to recognize so many of the names and more or less know what the cheerful descriptions were going to say.

There were a few birds he hadn't heard of, though: the *sooty shearwater*, a record-setting traveler during its yearly migration; the *ruddy turnstone*, with its harlequin markings; the *fork-tailed storm petrel*, which hunted out on the open ocean and mated for life. Jeremy stared at that last part for a while, thinking of the family from the lighthouse, and his own mom and dad, until a cluster of little kids surged over to rub their sticky hands on the displays and scream at the pictures.

Becker checked with a ranger as they were leaving the sanctuary, and from the sound of it, there wasn't much else worth visiting nearby. So, since they were already more than two hours away from the beach house, they decided to start back.

Jeremy's door crackled as they got into the truck, and his uncle looked over. "Hey, you haven't eaten your road trip fuel!" Becker said. "Get those gummies open, buddy!" Jeremy did as he was told, pulling out a water bottle from his pack to wash down the sugar. Becker chuckled. "What all do you have in that bag, anyway? Don't think you used any of it."

Jeremy showed him the contents, and Becker shook his head. "You sure got that *always be prepared* thing from your mom. Your dad *still* doesn't know how to pack for a road trip. Even when we were kids, I was the one bringing my allowance money for orange slices. Mike always forgot." He flicked on the radio as they reached the main road but kept the volume low. "Sorry there were all those tourists today, by the way," he said. "The coast's been getting busier every year. I guess it is Sunday, but it's usually quieter at these smaller places."

"There were so many families," said Jeremy. "Like, happy families." He hadn't meant to say the last part softly, but that was how it came out. Becker glanced over, then locked his eyes back on the road.

"You know," he said after a moment, "your dad really did love your mom, Jer. *Does*, I mean. Wait— That's not— I just . . ." He trailed off. The road hummed beneath them. "I'm trying to say Mike really cares about her, about both of you. He didn't want things to end up the way they did."

"I know that." Jeremy kept his head turned away. He could see his uncle reflected in the window.

"The thing you gotta remember is that this has nothing to do with you. All this change. Not one thing."

"Yeah."

Becker, reading his tone, let it drop. After a minute, he reached out to turn up the radio.

The billboards and fields and towns rolled by, and another hour's travel found Jeremy staring out the window again, the bird book tucked under his knee. He'd taken it out to study a while back, but flipping through the pages had made him miss Evan too much and he'd had to put it down.

He turned from the window and tapped his phone, hoping for a distraction. There were still no messages.

"Can people text when they're out on the ocean?" he asked.

Becker stopped his humming and shrugged. "Maybe? I dunno. Depends on where they are. Reception does funny things along the coast."

Jeremy nodded. At least he could still write messages himself. He debated for several miles whether to play it cool, but his heart was feeling heavy, and his brain was tired, and in the end, he just went ahead and shared.

> Hi! Went to a bird sanctuary up the coast with my uncle today. Kinda funny thing: two of the signs side by side read ANNOYING FRIENDS in our code.

> I learned about some cool new ones, too.

> The black-footed albatross lives its whole life out on the water. It never comes to land and barely ever sees others of its own kind.

> Actually that sounds super lonely. Maybe that's what black-footed albatross should mean?

> Hope you're having fun!

> Keep watching out for sharks!

> Get home safe.

Thirteen

Jeremy felt as if he and Uncle Becker had been gone for days by the time they got back to the beach house. It was strange to see everything looking just the same, with his dad still at the table surrounded by his papers and books.

His dad began talking the moment they walked in, telling them loudly about all the work he'd gotten done while Jeremy chugged two glasses of water and Becker helped himself to a beer.

"So, you gonna buy the house?" Jeremy's dad asked, finally. He'd grabbed a beer of his own, the vertical letters of *Mason's* flashing between his fingers.

Becker shook his head. "Nah, not my style."

"My brother, the world's pickiest beach-rental magnate."

"Hey, it was your son who pointed out the place didn't really fit together." Becker winked at his nephew. "He said it *didn't know what it was*. The boy's got a real flair for real estate."

Jeremy turned away as his father glanced at him. "I don't know where he picked that up. Anyway, it's probably good you're not taking it. You've got too many places already."

The conversation shifted to property development and taxes and insurance, and the two brothers fell into their usual chugging rhythm. Jeremy headed upstairs, unnoticed, and flopped back across his bed without turning on the light. The glow from the evening sky cast half the room in shadow, making the attic feel bigger, somehow—broader, more undefined at the edges.

He stared up at the ceiling. He had enjoyed his day with Uncle Becker, mostly because his uncle was different on his own: more thoughtful, more careful. Less like Jeremy's dad.

Thinking of his dad, the question of his own future housing arrangements came marching back into Jeremy's brain. He groaned, throwing an arm over his eyes, but the reality was this stay on the coast was ticking away, and he'd have to think about what was coming next sometime. Like it or not, Evan being gone was probably giving him his best chance to do that until they packed up their bags and drove away.

So, what did he want? Did he want to stick with the familiar and keep living in the family home with his dad? It would be an easier call in some ways, but not in others. Before the divorce, his dad had been the goofball, the rebel, the relaxer-in-chief; but judging from the last few months and his dad's attitude out here, that version of him didn't seem like it was coming back. So, what version of his dad would show up instead? His dad was clearly trying to figure out how to solo parent, when he managed to look up from his own work and worries, but so far it had all been pretty rough. Would the two of them find some balance back at the old house? Would his dad mellow out once they were settled? Or would Jeremy end up feeling like he was stuck living with only half a parent, someone who dished out plenty of boundaries but never any real support?

Getting nowhere, he switched, trying to imagine uprooting everything to live with his mom instead. He'd get plenty of attention that way, that was certain. Maybe too much. His mom had basically been parent-in-chief in the old family anyway, and he was willing to bet she would carry on exactly the same, arranging the world for him, organizing every minute, making sure he was optimizing his opportunities in his new city and school. It would be a lot to live with as he got older. But would it be better than life with his dad?

Maybe. It would be a change, at least. A big one. And how many times in his life would he get to make a choice that could have such a massive impact on his future?

Something told him it might just come down to how he felt about Beaverton and the new house when he went out there to visit. But shouldn't he base his decision on more important things? Shouldn't he have some clear and certain reason? Shouldn't he already know?

His thoughts went round and round in circles, Evan's face flashing among them, as the waves sighed against the shore and the seabirds cried and the last of the daylight faded into night.

The stars were out when he sat up, rubbing a crick in his neck. He tapped at his phone. Still no messages. None. Maybe it was just the ocean? Or maybe Evan was having the time of his life with his family and didn't need Jeremy anymore with his awkward silences and dorky texts.

Out of nowhere a shivering sense of urgency swept over Jeremy, and he thumbed out a sentence and hit send before he could think twice:

> If black-footed albatross = "lonely" then I'm totally black-footed albatross tonight, buddy.

His hands shook as he set down the phone.

The house had gone quiet, no TV buzz or brotherly bickering rumbling between the walls. Becker must have left. Jeremy skipped brushing his teeth, changed his clothes by starlight, and climbed into bed.

He almost felt like he was the one out at sea, drifting with the tide, looking back to land and wondering. He knew he had asked the universe a question in that last text. He could feel it all around him in the silence. And he would have to wait to have it answered.

When sleep came, Jeremy dreamed he was on a ferry navigating the deep green waters between the islands off Seattle, a journey his family had made in real life the summer he was seven. He dreamed of the vinyl benches deep enough to sleep on; the windows with their rounded corners; the white and green and midnight paint; the foggy blast of the horn.

He was alone in the dream and lost, searching the empty boat, calling out for someone, anyone to hear him. Terror was scratching at his heels when a tawny doe appeared, picking her way delicately up the stairs from the lower car deck. He stopped dead, and so did she, her dark eyes holding his for a single breath, and then all the staircases were pouring with deer. They came running along the aisles, leaping over seats, charging through the galley past the bags of chips and coffeepots, driving as one toward the front of the ferry.

Jeremy followed, pushing with the warm wave of bodies out onto the viewing deck, into the cold wind, out to where an island lay ahead under a glowing sky. There were houses on the island with lights in their windows, and gulls wheeling above the shore, and a crowd of smiling people waiting on the dock to meet them, the herd of deer and the boy, who for some reason in his dream had started crying.

When the day returned, Jeremy woke to seven texts from Evan.

Fourteen

MONDAY, JULY 2

When he was very little, Jeremy had woken each day to the sound of his mother's voice. Every morning, she would tiptoe into his room singing a wake-up song, one hand brushing his shoulder as she sat on the edge of his bed. Then they would talk, the two of them. She would tell him about all the important things they had to do that day, and he would tell her about his dreams if he remembered them, his mother nodding along even though they never made any sense. It was always the same, a few shared moments to start the day. He'd tried once or twice to remember when those visits had stopped, or why, but only came up with empty air.

Waking to Evan's texts brought the feeling of those mornings rushing back. The comfort of someone reaching out. Being right there.

Hey! Sorry went to bed. Have to get up SO EARLY for fishing

Ugh it's gross now why am I awake

Guess what we caught yesterday? No-th-ing

Cousins are super annoyed. Uncle says that's not why we're out here but you know

Hope stuff with your uncle was good. You gonna go running today?

The last were sent fifteen minutes later.

And hey sorry you're black-footed albatross dude

Marbled murrelet, marbled murrelet, marbled murrelet

Jeremy had to think for a second to remember what that last one meant in the language of seabirds: *friends, friends, friends.* He lay back, his arms flopping wide. Hearing from Evan was like breathing air again after centuries of being underwater.

He raised his phone to read the line of texts over, and then over again, wondering if he would ever stop smiling. One thing was certain: Now that Evan had brought it up for the second time, he absolutely *would* be going running on his own. Just to prove he could.

He put off the run until evening, when most of the tourists were crowded into restaurants and the beach was as empty as it was going to get, calling a goodbye to his dad, who was wearing an apron and staring grumpily into the fridge.

Starting turned out to be difficult on his own. His old awkwardness was back, and he tripped just going down the porch steps. Even the sand felt different somehow, dense and heavy on his shoes, and there was an uncomfortable warm-up period where he couldn't get his breathing to settle into any sort of rhythm.

Eventually he managed it, his heart and lungs slipping into time with his feet. He made his way south, doing his best to avoid the inevitable knots of people, until the beach opened up and it was just him and the birds and the wind. He plodded along, letting the steady movement blur away the tangles filling his brain, only stopping when his eyes landed on a familiar-looking log beside a curve of dark pebbles.

He dropped to a walk and headed over, panting and shaking his head in surprise. This was where he'd thrown up on his very first run! That had been only, what, four days ago? And now here he was again, after the same almost-two miles, doing pretty good. Okay, he'd gone a whole lot slower, and he still had to lean on his knees to breathe, but he had some energy left this time. And he sure wasn't adding his lunch to the sand.

He straightened suddenly and, before he could think, resumed his run. One more curve of the beach, just to see if he could. And maybe another. It would be something to tell Evan.

In the end, he ran three more curves, right up to where the beach swooped sharply inland under the sixty-foot-high walls of Marbletop Cliffs. The sun was low, the tide heading out, and almost by instinct he began searching the fresh wet sand, turning up three pieces of beach glass—two frosty clear, one brown—four dead fish, a near-perfect sand dollar, and a bottle cap with a picture of a deer on it.

Jeremy was genuinely surprised at himself. He should have been tired, but instead he felt buzzingly alive, the burn in his lungs working on him like a tonic, and he prowled the sand with a fierce, restless energy he decided he could definitely get used to.

Was this what change felt like? Good change? Growing change? A week ago, he wouldn't have dreamed of going running on his own, and now he'd done it. Just like that.

Jeremy breathed in the cold, briny wind, smiling out at the sea. Evan would be proud of him for this.

He ran home with the peach-blush light of early sunset, his heart so bright he felt like he was running on clouds. Past the curves, along the beach, and there was the roof, his window, the porch.

He pounded up the steps and was about to open the door when the sight of the white shells on the railing stopped him. He squinted, tapping his thumbs against his fingers. It was Monday again. It had been Monday when they arrived. One of their two weeks was gone. He hefted the closest shell and set it free, soaring back to the beach.

Inside, he found his father stretched out in the living room watching a movie.

"You missed dinner," said his father, his eyes not moving from the screen.

"Oh." Jeremy wiped a wrist across his forehead. "Yeah, sorry. I went out pretty far."

His father made no response. An explosion filled the TV, its glare flashing on the bottle in his hand, the line of beer sloshing just under the *o* in *Mason's*. The clock ticked, and Jeremy felt the warmth on his skin beginning to fade. "There's pasta in the fridge," his father finally grunted.

"Thanks." Jeremy turned for the kitchen.

"Hold it."

Jeremy stopped. "Yeah?"

"Shower first, please. Don't need you grossing up the kitchen."

"Oh." Jeremy looked down, seeing himself through his dad's eyes. The last of his happy glow winked out, and he headed for the bathroom.

The fluorescent light and bathroom mirror showed him a sweaty kid with a face so pink and splotchy even his freckles were missing. He showered quickly, then stepped back into the blue TV glow of the living room, his clothes in his arms and a towel around his waist.

His dad raised his beer bottle in salute, or maybe just acknowledgment, and Jeremy saw the foamy line was now sloshing under the letter *a*. Higher than it was before.

He lined up what that meant before he reached the top of the stairs.

Later, after he'd eaten his dinner and done the dishes, he headed barefoot down to the waterline. There was no one else around, just an old couple walking their dog away along the sand. The waves sounded different at night, as if the darkness was reflecting their swoosh and roar back to them, the echoes disappearing under the foam.

Jeremy paced, feeling a bit like the human version of the lime-green house: not quite fitting together right, not fitting in anywhere he wanted to settle. Except for running, of course. That had been glorious. Now that it was over, his head felt heavy, crowded with thoughts about his mom and the divorce, about his dad and his beer, about running and reaching and trying on purpose. About Evan. And the future. And Evan.

The rumble of his phone in his pocket made him jump, then scramble for it. He was practically in the Pacific Ocean, foam licking around his toes. Only one person's texts could reach that far.

Hey! SUPER good day. Hit our catch quota early

And oldest cousin has a date or something, plus another two are arguing

So yeah, anyway, just got home

Jeremy stared at the glowing rectangle in his hands. A wave washed over his feet, but he didn't notice. He didn't breathe. Not until the next text came through.

Wanna hang out?

Fifteen

Evan was coming over.

Jeremy had replied. Evan had texted back. And now Evan was coming over.

Panicking in advance, Jeremy had sent a warning about not waking up his dad and the danger of the squeaky stairs. The reply—*Will just climb porch then*—had pinged in almost immediately, and he'd had to walk five laps around his room to calm down before settling in to wait in the open window, his arms around his knees, feeling poised on the very edge of his life.

At last, he caught the sound of footsteps around the side of the house, the *thunk* of shoes on the porch railing, a muffled grunt of effort—and then Evan was there, crawling up onto the roof.

Jeremy felt himself beaming, so happy he thought the light from his bedside lamp must be shining right through him. "Hey," he whispered.

"Hey." Evan was smiling, too, and Jeremy felt a tug somewhere behind his belly button.

He moved out of the window as Evan clambered in, tossing a paper grocery bag at the foot of Jeremy's bed. Evan looked around.

"Cool room. All this stuff yours?"

"Not the furniture; that's my uncle's. The rest is mine."

Evan gave himself a tour, eyeing the neatly stacked clothes, peering at the pine boards, scanning the titles of the books Jeremy had brought. He seemed genuinely curious, and Jeremy stood watching the inspection, unsure how to feel. Was Evan curious about the beach house? The attic room? Him?

"So, hey," Jeremy said, settling cross-legged on the floor with his back against the bed, hoping he looked cool and relaxed. "How was the ocean?"

Evan finished measuring his height against the angled ceiling and came over, flopping down beside Jeremy in the puddle of lamplight.

"It was really good." He leaned back on his hands. "I mean, the fishing was great, once it got going. Obviously, since we hit our quota and came back early. And there was some, uh, family stuff with my cousins that went well. I was happy about that."

"Nice! What age are your cousins again?"

"All older. The ones who come on this trip are in high school. They always used to treat me like a little kid, since I'm the family baby, but I guess they think I'm old enough now. Pretty sure this was the first time they've ever actually listened to me." He picked a pill of fabric off the rug and rolled it between his fingers, seeming to drift away for a second. "Anyway, it was good! What about you? You been running? How was hanging out with your uncle?"

"What? You can't just be done like that!" Jeremy was grinning. He couldn't help it. Evan was right here in his bedroom, talking with him, hanging out. "You didn't tell a single shark story."

"We didn't see any sharks. Can't tell a shark story if we didn't see any sharks."

"Well, make one up, then."

"Only if you tell me about shopping for houses with your uncle."

"Deal."

"Deal."

So Jeremy told Evan about touring the lime-green house with Becker, and about the lighthouse and the bird sanctuary, and his solo run on the beach; and Evan made up a surprisingly good story about a shark eating his cousins and sneaking on land wearing all their clothes at once.

"Hey, that reminds me," Evan said, leaning over to grab the paper grocery bag.

"Oh, is that food?" asked Jeremy. "I can run down and get some of ours, too, if you want. Or some plates and napkins."

"It's not food." Evan dropped the bag into Jeremy's arms—it was heavy. "It's a present. And no, I'm good on food. I mean, if you are."

Jeremy stayed very still, holding the crinkling bag like a living thing. A present? For him? From Evan?

Evan flipped over to lie on his stomach, pulling his phone from his pocket. "Open it," he said, tapping at the screen. A moment later, classical music poured into the room, a sweet, sad blend of piano and strings that made Jeremy think of moonlight.

Slowly, he unfolded the brown paper bag and looked inside. He heard his own sharp inhale. His head snapped up.

Evan was watching him from under his lashes.

Terror seared through Jeremy. He felt stripped bare. The shame of being caught—seen—discovered—crawled over his skin. It took everything he had not to smash the bag shut and hurl it out the window.

His hands shook as he slid the contents into the light: eight copies of *Vogue* and a *Vanity Fair*.

"Hey, whoa . . . are you—are you okay?" asked Evan, his eyes widening as he spotted Jeremy's expression. "I thought you'd maybe like them! I got them with the money my grandma pays me for watching the shop. I can take them back if you—"

"No!"

Jeremy shook his head, reeling as Evan's words made it through the storm in his brain. It was all right, somehow. "No, these—these are amazing. Thank you. I just . . . you saw me?"

Evan nodded.

"Right from the start? I mean, you knew?"

A nod.

"And it's . . . okay?"

A smile. Another nod.

Jeremy looked back at the stack of treasure in his hands. "Thank you," he said again.

Evan had known. Evan had watched him reach for the magazines and seen through his lies that very first day. And Evan had still wanted to get to know him. Had still wanted to be his friend.

What should he say now? How did you tell someone they'd just given you the best gift of your entire life?

He rubbed a hand over his face.

"Seriously, are you okay?" Evan asked.

"Totally." Jeremy bobbed his head. "Thank you, is all. I mean it. This was super nice of you."

"It's fine." Evan pushed himself up on his elbows. "But now you have to show me what the deal is with this stuff."

"What stuff?"

"This." Evan grabbed a magazine. "Dresses. Giant pants. Fashion. What makes it cool?"

"Oh." Jeremy blinked. "I mean, you just kind of look at it? And decide if you like it?"

"But I want to know why *you* like it. You obviously have, like, an eye. You picked out those awesome running shoes. Show me more."

Evan was busy flipping pages, and didn't see the color climbing up Jeremy's neck.

"I've, um, never talked to anyone about this, but . . ." Jeremy opened the nearest *Vogue* and scooched around, angling it between them. "Okay, see this crimson jacket with the puffy satin sleeves? Start there."

"Jacket. Crimson. Puffy satin sleeves. Check."

"Well, it's fancy, right?" Jeremy paused, gathering his thoughts. "Okay, so imagine wearing it."

Evan laughed but nodded.

"Think about how it would make you feel." Jeremy felt incredibly awkward but kind of giddy, too. "How would you walk down the street if you were wearing that, or into a room? It would be different, right, compared to how you walk around in a T-shirt? You'd probably move differently? And people would notice?"

Evan was squinting at the picture. He nodded again.

"I think—I think that's what I like about fashion: the way it changes how you can feel. Or more like what you can *say*. The clothes they put in here are usually saying something big." He flipped through another magazine, stopping at a model in a pale green Cinderella-style gown and fleece-lined denim jacket leaning against a motorcycle.

"Okay, this, right here." He moved a bit closer to Evan. "This is a serious look, right? If you walked into a room wearing this, it would mean something, and people would get that. This outfit would tell them who you are, and what you think about yourself, and what you think about the world. And it would do that all by itself, partly because of the cut and color and everything, but mostly because you chose it." He could hear the energy rising in his voice. He wondered suddenly if he was talking too much.

Evan was smile-frowning at the photograph. "I think I get it!" he said. "It's why they say something is a fashion statement, right?" He ran a finger over the model and the motorcycle. "This one's really romantic."

Jeremy felt as though he'd tumbled off a ladder again as Evan's words sent his insides lurching in two directions at once.

On one hand, it was wildly distracting to hear Evan say the word *romantic* when they were sitting so close together right here in his bedroom. On the other, he couldn't help noticing how Evan's eyes were lingering over the model. Jeremy was drawn to fashion magazines for the clothes, and the glamour, and the impossible dream of a life where being that grand and visible was something safe to want. But it looked as though Evan was finding something else to like, maybe, in these pages of beautiful women.

Jeremy swallowed hard, searching for a distraction. "Yeah, it is romantic. Kind of like your music." He tilted his head at Evan's phone. "I mean, I don't know much, but it sounds that way to me?"

"Hey, yeah, totally!" Evan pointed a finger at him. "So clothes can have feelings the same way music does. Good comparison, teach." He reached for another magazine, rested his chin on his hands, and began reading.

Proud, uncertain, embarrassed, and happy, Jeremy settled down to join him.

Outside, the waves rolled on under the turning stars, while inside the attic the two boys flipped through shirts and dresses and makeup ads, the light from the bedside lamp pooling around them, their quiet voices weaving together like birds in the air.

Sixteen

TUESDAY, JULY 3

"Higher, Evan! Higher—no, not that high!"

It was just after six the next evening, and Gloria, in a fluorescent-pink dress and floral sun hat, stood on the sidewalk in front of Tidepool Knickknacks, directing Jeremy and Evan through the surprisingly complicated task of getting the store's new vinyl banner level.

Evan waved over at Jeremy from his ladder. "You know this isn't for *this* Fourth of July, right, Jeremy? We're starting early for next year."

"Quiet," said Gloria. "We would have been finished by now if you two had just followed my instructions. Okay, down a bit, Jeremy, and, Evan, you go up. No, wait, I mean the other way around."

Eventually, somehow, they did it. The banner was hung, ladders were returned to the shops they'd been borrowed from, and the three of them stood on the sidewalk admiring their work amid the crowds of dinnertime tourists.

A TIDEPOOL OF GOOD WISHES
THIS FOURTH OF JULY
FROM OUR FAMILY TO YOURS

"That's really nice, Gloria," Jeremy said.

"Yeah." Evan had his head to one side. "And it'll totally make people want to come in and buy knickknacks. Patriotic *and* confusing? Perfect advertising."

Jeremy laughed as Gloria prodded her grandson in pretend annoyance, but his mind was stuck on the words swaying in the breeze: *From our family to yours.*

He didn't really have a family to receive the *Tidepool of Good Wishes* this year. In the old days, he and his parents had always gone to see the city fireworks, oohing and aahing along with crowds of other people picnicking on blankets just like them. One memorable year, his dad smuggled a pack of sparklers home afterward, pulling eight-year-old Jeremy out of bed so they could light them in secret behind the garage. Of course, his mom had caught them, though to his and his dad's surprise she'd let them continue, standing off to the side with the hose running in case, unable to keep down her smile.

It wasn't much, as family traditions went, but it had been something. What would the Fourth be like now? Would he have to split the holiday between his parents, alternating year after year? That might make it hard to keep up any kind of traditions. Would it all come down to him?

"Hey, dreamer!"

Jeremy startled. Gloria was waving to him from the door of the shop. "I said, do you want a soda?"

"Please! Thank you!" The day was hot, and as he leaned against the side of the shop beside Evan, Jeremy realized how thirsty he was.

Gloria reappeared. "Only one cold one," she said, passing an open glass bottle to Evan. "You boys will have to share."

Jeremy jumped like the side of the building had burned him. "That's okay!" Was he talking too loudly? He might be talking too loudly. "I'm fine, really! Evan should have it."

Hanging out and talking fashion magazines was one thing, but drinking from the same soda bottle? That was a whole other level. That was almost like . . .

"Don't be silly! You both worked hard. And Evan will be happy to share with his guest, correct?"

"Course." Evan held the bottle out to Jeremy. He took it, feeling the condensation on the cold glass, the warmth of Evan's fingertips just grazing his.

"Well, we're all done here," said Gloria. "You two were such a help!" She locked the store behind her and dropped the keys in her bag. "I've got a date tonight, so don't wait up! Oh, yoo-hoo!"

Jeremy and Evan turned to where she was waving and saw Mr. Sharma, all fancied up in suspenders and crisp ironed slacks, beaming like a kid from his side of the street.

"Never hesitate on love, my darlings," Gloria called, one hand holding down her sun hat as she danced over to meet her date. "It's nothing but a waste of time!"

Evan cleared his throat as the old people disappeared into the crowd, and Jeremy, guessing he was embarrassed over his grandma, gave him a smile.

"Cool," Evan said. "Hey, would you, uh, wanna go up to Lookout Park? We could just hang out? Talk, maybe? That be okay?"

Jeremy nodded, although the questions left him confused. Apart from running, they always just hung out and talked. Why did Evan suddenly think he had to ask?

They headed up the street, the sun on their backs, the icy soda passing between them. Jeremy's heart fluttered every time he took the bottle and brought it to his lips. It was so intense but so casual at the same time. He kept wanting to shake his head that a moment like this could just *happen* out here on the coast. To him. In his actual life. Without him even trying.

They finished the soda as they reached the steps leading to the park, and it took everything Jeremy had not to go diving after the bottle when Evan tossed it into a recycling bin. If there'd been any chance of hiding it, he would have kept it forever as a souvenir.

Lookout Park was set on a bluff above Rosemont's shopping district, and it was already crowded. All the benches and tables were occupied, even the sand around the slides, so Jeremy and Evan settled down on one of the logs marking the park's edge, facing out west toward the sea.

Neither of them said anything at first. Jeremy felt wonderful. He was still glowing from the walk, and the view was spectacular, and the sugar from the soda was zinging through his veins. He couldn't stop smiling.

But as the minutes rolled by, he became aware that the silence he and Evan were sitting in was different this time. He glanced over, but Evan had his head turned slightly away, staring out at the horizon.

A shadow of worry slanted across Jeremy's good mood. Evan had been the one who'd said he wanted to talk. Why was he being so quiet?

"Hey, so are your grandma and Mr. Sharma, you know, a couple?" Jeremy asked, just to kick things off. It felt a little weird—he usually followed Evan's lead.

Evan had his elbows propped on his knees, tangling and untangling his fingers. He nodded. "Yeah, they've been dating."

"That's cool," said Jeremy.

"Yep."

"Mr. Sharma's pretty easy to like."

"Mm-hmm."

The nervous silence returned. They stared out over the town.

Worry trickled into Jeremy's mind, rising with each passing second. This must be because of him. He must have slipped up. Had he been too obvious about the soda bottle? Smiled when he shouldn't have? Given everything away? He felt the familiar beginnings of fear at whatever Evan wasn't saying.

"I liked what your grandma said about not waiting on love," he blurted out, trying again with the same topic. "My uncle thinks that, too, but says it kind of different. He says life doesn't start until you've got a girlfriend." He stopped, feeling like his throat was closing up. Evan had his face turned completely away now. What was happening?

Jeremy doubled down. "I mean, it's not like I want one yet. A girlfriend, I mean. Someday. But I'm not even good at keeping regular friends yet." He forced himself to laugh. The sound of it hurt his ears.

He was panicking, babbling nonsense, saying things he didn't even mean. But he was so scared at the change in Evan. Why were his shoulders hunching in like that? Why was he clenching his hands?

Jeremy cleared his throat, swallowed, cleared his throat again, as happy voices filled the park around them.

In one sudden motion, Evan got to his feet. "Sorry!" he said. "Sorry, I know I said we should come up here, but I think I actually need to move."

"Oh." Jeremy scrambled up beside him. "Okay."

"Do you play soccer? Want to go down to the beach and kick a ball around or something?"

"Sure! Yes!" Jeremy would have said yes to anything so long as Evan wanted to keep hanging out.

"Nice. We can grab one from my place on the way." Evan started back down the hill, cutting through the long grass toward the road. "And hey, Jeremy?" he said, without turning. "I think you're great at keeping friends." He walked on a few more paces. "I mean, you're pretty easy to like, too."

Jeremy stumbled, catching his balance just in time to avoid tumbling at Evan's feet. He couldn't think of a single thing to say, as his brain had gone to pieces, but Evan didn't seem to be expecting a reply. Jeremy followed his friend back toward the shops, baffled now as well as anxious, but grateful to the soles of his feet to be leaving whatever Evan had left unsaid behind them.

They had just turned onto Main Street when Jeremy heard a grown-up voice calling his name. He looked around, puzzled, and jerked to a stop at the sight of his father and Uncle Becker waving at them from the other side of the street.

"Who's that?" asked Evan, stopping beside him.

"Um, my dad." Jeremy's heart was racing. Why did this have to happen now, when things with Evan were only just feeling okay again? "And my uncle."

"Oh, cool." Evan raised a hand and waved back.

The two men headed over, cutting through the slow tourist traffic. Jeremy's dad was wearing his aviator sunglasses again. Jeremy couldn't read his expression.

"Hey, Jer!" said Becker, grinning as he reached them. "Who've we got here?"

Evan held out a hand. "Hi, I'm Evan. Evan Sandford."

"Becker Ryden, Jeremy's uncle." They shook.

"Mike, his father," said Jeremy's dad, and he and Evan shook, too.

Jeremy stood to the side, awkward and silent.

"So, are you a local?" his dad asked Evan. "You and Jeremy just meet?"

"I spend summers here," Evan answered. He glanced over at Jeremy. "But we've been hanging out for almost a week now. We go on runs and stuff."

Jeremy's dad pulled off his sunglasses. "Wait, you've been running with a friend this whole time, Jer?" His eyebrows knotted. "Why didn't you say? How come you haven't invited him over to the house?"

Jeremy flushed, remembering the night before, with Evan sprawled in a pile of magazines on his bedroom floor. "I just, um, haven't gotten around to it yet." He kept his gaze fixed over his dad's shoulder, but he still saw Evan's look of surprise. This whole situation was becoming way too complicated. He felt sweat running down his back.

"Huh," said his dad. "Well, that's kind of weird. Obviously, you're gonna have to bring your new friend to the party tomorrow."

Jeremy finally looked at his father. "The . . . party?"

"Yeah! I'm throwing a party! For the Fourth, obviously, but also 'cause your uncle here is leaving the day after to work on his properties up the coast. Won't be back until the day we leave, he says! He's calling all his friends to come tomorrow; should be fun." He looked happier at the idea than Jeremy had seen him in months. "Of course," his dad went on, "the first year I'm allowed to shoot fireworks again, and I can't find anything better than snap-its left in this whole darn town!"

"He's making me search store to store with him to see what else we can find," said Becker, rolling his eyes. "Which is such an obvious excuse to end up at Sandy's Grill I'm embarrassed to call him my brother."

He dodged away as Jeremy's dad punched him on the shoulder.

"So, we'll see you tomorrow, yeah, Evan?" Becker said, grinning. "You've gotta be there. Jer's gonna need at least one friend his own age to hang out with!"

Jeremy wondered how many ways there were to melt into the

pavement from embarrassment, but Evan nodded. "It sounds like fun. Thanks."

"Okay, come on, Becks." Jeremy's dad pulled his sunglasses back on. "Clock's ticking, and we are not going home empty-handed. There's gotta be decent fireworks left for sale somewhere around here."

With nods and waves, the Ryden men headed off, leaving Jeremy and Evan by themselves again on the bustling sidewalk.

"They seem nice," said Evan. He turned, quirking his mouth at Jeremy. "Hey, why didn't you tell your dad about me?"

Jeremy looked down, becoming intensely interested in a dandelion growing out of a crack in the sidewalk. "No reason." He prodded the flower with his shoe. "My dad can just get pretty, you know, *Heermann's gull* sometimes. I guess I wanted to keep things kind of . . . separate."

"Like, a secret?"

"No!" said Jeremy, way too aware of how *secret* could sound. "Only, there's stuff I share with him and stuff I want to keep to myself, is all." He was sweating again. The dandelion pollen was yellowing up his shoe.

"Oh, okay. I get it," said Evan. There was something like a grin in his voice. "You want to keep me all to yourself."

Jeremy jerked his head up, mortified, but Evan, grinning for real, tilted his own head in the direction of Tidepool Knickknacks and started walking, his final words tugging Jeremy after him.

"That's cool."

Seventeen

WEDNESDAY, JULY 4

The Fourth of July arrived like an ad from the Oregon coast tourism board. Flags snapped under a perfectly blue sky, the grocery store put out a popcorn stand covered in stars-and-stripes rosettes, and everywhere there were excited, smiling people counting down the hours until nightfall, when they could send up the fireworks.

The feeling of excitement seeped into Jeremy's skin as he made his final trip into town for party supplies. After a midmorning grocery run for meat, chips, and a cart or two of alcohol, Jeremy's dad had put himself in charge of building a music playlist and setting up the bonfire. That had left Jeremy to spend his own afternoon slowly tidying the house, taking breaks now and then to walk into town for the odds and ends his dad had forgotten.

He didn't really mind. Evan was busy working, since there were too many tourists for the knickknack shop to close for the holiday, and the easy, low-key errands were good for filling up the time. Plus, he was enjoying being part of the general bustle. From old couples rolling carts full of soda and potato chips through the grocery store, to yapping dogs dressed up as Uncle Sam, to parents arguing with bawling toddlers over how late they were allowed to stay up—every bit of celebration added a welcome, communal glow to Jeremy's first post-divorce Fourth.

He made himself an early dinner from the party food when he returned from his final trip, and by the time the sun began sliding toward the horizon, he was antsy with expectation. Something big was going to happen tonight; he knew it. He wanted it to happen. He wanted the night to start. He wanted Evan to be there. He wanted to run.

Finally, finally, his phone buzzed with a text saying Evan was heading over. Jeremy thumbed back a reply, tossed his phone onto his bed, and sprinted down to the porch to wait.

He'd been pacing and stretching for five minutes when his dad, coming in from the unlit bonfire on the beach, spotted him.

"Whoa, whoa, whoa!" he said, stomping up the steps. "That ain't no party outfit, Jer. You think you're going somewhere?"

"Um, yeah," said Jeremy. "Evan and I decided to go for a run. Before the fireworks and stuff?"

His father's mouth tightened. "Oh, you decided that, did you? Well, your uncle and our other guests will be getting here any minute. I was counting on you to help out."

"I will," Jeremy said, wishing he could point out that he'd already spent half his day cleaning the house. "Later. It's not like we're going to go watch movies all night or something. I just want to hang out with my friend for a bit first."

His father crossed his arms. "It seems like you've spent most of your time here with this friend already. Something I only found out yesterday, by the way! Tonight should be about family."

The little spark of anger inside Jeremy woke again at that. This was his dad's idea of family time? A party with a bunch of grown-ups neither of them knew? "It's just a run!" he said. "We'll be right back. No one will notice I'm gone."

His father looked ready to keep arguing, but then footsteps came crunching through the sand behind them and there was Evan, already pink from running and smiling his unstoppable smile.

"Hi, Mr. Ryden," he said, waving. "Thanks again for inviting me. Happy Fourth!"

Jeremy's dad nodded. "Happy Fourth. Jeremy tells me you two are going on one of your runs."

"Yeah." Evan turned his smile on Jeremy. "He's helping me stay on top of my cross-country training. It's been really great."

Jeremy blushed at him.

"Wait, you say you run cross-country?" Jeremy's dad's face changed, his arms unfolding. "I did track back in high school before I switched to baseball! What kind of times are you getting?"

The two of them began chatting happily about fast starts and distance training, and within thirty seconds, Jeremy knew he had won.

"Don't be too late!" his dad called from the porch a few minutes later as he and Evan set off. "There's a box of sparklers I got special with your name on it, Jer!"

Jeremy gave a wave, but he was barely listening. Not one part of him was thinking about the party. All he wanted was to be alone with Evan, racing across the sand.

It seemed like the whole town was spread out across the beach. They ran past sunbathing families, barbecue grills, bonfires, coolers, barking dogs, babies with balloons, kids with kites, and knots of shouting teenagers, all ready and eager for what was to come.

Jeremy could not believe how good it felt to run now. His lungs still burned and his legs still ached, but something inside him had opened up, broadened and stretched, and there were long moments when the feel of his feet moving across the sand was almost like flying. He pushed himself, leaning into the feeling as he and Evan left the crowds behind, feeding off the energy of the day and the anticipation of the night.

They ran and ran, the land to their left growing steeper as they followed the familiar curves of beach into new territory, past the wet sand mouth of the cove carving inland under Marbletop Cliffs, out onto the rocky flats beyond, alone with the birds and the oncoming sunset.

Jeremy was exhausted by the time Evan called a halt, but still almost sorry to be stopping.

They walked in circles, panting, hands braced behind their necks. "Good job—on the run," Evan said. "You're getting—solid." He whapped Jeremy on the arm. "Hey! Look, look—look!"

"What?"

Evan pounced forward, scrabbling in the sand, then held something out to Jeremy, dark grains clinging to his fingers.

Jeremy took it and rubbed his thumb over a smooth, frosty blue-green triangle. "Turquoise beach glass," he said. His stomach flipped, then flipped again. He beamed at Evan. "Think it's a lucky sign?"

Evan stood. "Definitely. Now you have to find me a green one."

Jeremy tried, but a search of their resting spot found nothing more interesting than a snarl of plastic bendy straws and two dead jellyfish. He gave up and went to join Evan, who was leaning against a pitted driftwood log, and they sprawled out side by side, resting their legs and watching the sun settle over the waves.

The feeling of anticipation was still there, quieter now but more intense. Jeremy felt it building in his palms and behind his ears as the sun dropped. He and Evan were sitting close, and he could feel the heat radiating off his friend as the wind cooled his own sweat-soaked shirt.

They watched, holding on to that silence until the last bright flash of sunset disappeared below the waterline.

Evan stirred. "We better go," he said. "It'll be close to dark when we get back."

They stood, shaking out their legs and feet, and Jeremy was surprised to see the water was higher than he'd thought. Their view from the log and the glare of the sun had fooled him. He looked over in time to see Evan frown, and they set out, Evan quickly picking up the pace.

Within two minutes, Jeremy was flagging. He patted the pocket with his new beach glass, trying to resummon that wild, driving energy he'd felt on the way out.

But the turquoise glass was gone.

"Hey! Wait!" He pulled to an awkward, stumbling halt. "I lost it!"

"What?" Evan looked back, then stopped, too.

"The piece of glass—you gave me. Must have fallen out on the log!"

Evan waved a hand. "It's fine! You'll find a new one."

"No—it's not fine!" Jeremy felt more heat rising to his sweating face. "It's really—I have to get it!" Their log was still in sight. He turned back.

"Dude, we don't have time!" yelled Evan. But Jeremy kept on, and a moment later he heard Evan's shoes hitting the sand behind him.

They reached the log together. Jeremy found the glass right where he'd been sitting and had to fight the urge to press it to his lips, holding it up triumphantly instead.

"Great," said Evan. "Now, seriously—we have to go. This tide's coming up fast. No lagging."

They ran in silence, the wind whuffling in their ears and curls of sundried seaweed skittering past their ankles. The glowing twilight shone back at itself from the rising sea, and Jeremy quickly became aware of two very important things: He wouldn't be able to keep up this pace for the rest of their return journey, and they still had to get past the cove under Marbletop Cliffs.

"Evan." All strength was gone from Jeremy's voice, and he had to call again to make Evan look back.

"We gotta go!" Evan panted, still running.

"I know!" Jeremy gave a grunt of effort and sped up to reach his side. "But maybe we should—get off the beach and—just walk back—over the cliffs?"

Evan shook his head. "That would mean going back first to get up—and around. And way more distance to get home." He squinted between the sea and the shore. "We've got this."

They ran on, the waves eating their way toward them, the sand shortening as they passed the southern arm of the cove. On their way out, they had cut across from one arm to another like the string of a bow. Now the rising sea was forcing them to head inland, following the rocky curve around its edge, making their way longer. Much longer. Evan sped up.

The sky was fading from gold to indigo, and Jeremy's lungs were rattling like broken beer bottles in his chest, when he realized they weren't going to make it.

Evan gasped beside him, his arms and legs pumping, but the sea had them pushed right up against the mountain of logs and knotted kelp piled along the cliff base. Stray branches reached out to trip them. The wet sand sucked at their shoes. And half the long curve of the cove still lay ahead.

Jeremy stumbled to a stop, a shard from his broken-bottle lungs lodging as a stitch in his side. He clutched at it, sucking in air through clenched teeth. "Evan!"

Evan was still trying to run. He took two more steps, then jumped back, swearing, as his shoes splashed into cold water. He climbed up onto a gnarled log and stared out at the sea swallowing their escape route, his eyes wide.

"What do we do?" Jeremy croaked. "We're trapped!" Uncle Becker's words from his first day on the coast rang through his mind: *You get stuck out there when the tide comes in, you better either be a real strong swimmer or else know how to fly.*

Swimming was obviously out of the question if the tide was able to throw these giant logs around. No amount of kicking would keep them safe in that. And as for flying? Jeremy looked up. Seabirds circled the cliffs, riding the sunset wind, unaware and uncaring that far below them two boys were stuck between a hard stone wall and the cold, breaking sea. Two boys who would have given anything to join them.

Jeremy scrambled onto a log of his own, then up to another, but the surf and foam were already submerging both. Horror gripped him as he climbed higher, a nightmare comprehension that the Pacific Ocean was rolling in exactly where he was standing and he couldn't turn it aside or get himself out of its way. He felt a desperate urge to flail his arms or hurl a rock or shout, as if any of that might make the ocean change its course or hold back its heaving strength.

"Jeremy! Here!"

Jeremy's trance broke. Evan was at his side, tugging at his arm, hauling him up the debris pile to press against the jagged wall of the cliff.

"What are—" he began, but Evan interrupted.

"Just follow! Don't think! And don't look down!"

Jeremy did as he was told.

He followed Evan along the topmost ridge of slippery, teetering logs.

He followed as Evan turned to the wall and began to climb, his clenched fingers and wet shoes scrabbling for holds in the sun-warmed stone.

He followed and he didn't think as Evan somehow disappeared

above him, leaving Jeremy clinging alone ten feet above the logs with sea spray prickling his back.

He didn't think and he didn't look down as Evan's hands reappeared, grabbing at his elbows, his shoulders, his shirt, hauling him onto a narrow ledge in the rock not quite big enough for two.

He didn't look down as he and Evan pressed into each other and the cliff, tangled, scraped, and gasping.

When his breathing finally slowed, and Jeremy finally looked . . .

. . . he saw nothing but sea beneath them.

Eighteen

"You mean we're stuck here for six entire hours?" Jeremy asked.

They were back-to-back on the ledge on the cliff face, their shirts clinging to them, arms wrapped around their legs for warmth. Jeremy was grateful he'd stopped shaking—and even more grateful Evan had remembered how to find their narrow shelf of safety.

Once the initial terror was over, Evan had told Jeremy how he'd found the ledge two summers before when the log pile was higher, guessing from the lichen and moss it must be above the high tide line. He'd remembered it only just in time, though it was far from an ideal spot. They had room, barely, if they stayed hunched up, but with the wall of rock looming above and the short sheer drop into the water below, Jeremy felt like he was going to fall at any second. And they had a long cold wait ahead.

"Six hours at least," said Evan. Jeremy could feel the rumble of his voice against his back. "We'll have to wait till the tide's low enough to splash back to land in the dark. Plus, those logs are gonna be super dangerous, so we'll have to go slow." He huffed a laugh. "Maybe we should have brought our phones for this one. We're definitely not making it to your dad's party."

Jeremy let out a laugh of his own. Setting aside the cold and the danger and the fear, being this close to Evan was still better than any beach party could ever be.

"That's really okay," he said. "But are you gonna be in trouble with your grandma if you don't get home until late?"

"Can't do anything about it," said Evan. "I'll just have to explain in the morning."

The last faint gleam of sunset still clung to the western sky, but full dark was on its way. Jeremy shivered and felt that tingle behind his ears again that had nothing to do with cold. The night was awake, somehow, alive—and so was he.

"Hey, so, um, why'd you go back?" asked Evan suddenly. "It's totally my fault we got stuck; I should have been paying more attention. But why was"—he cleared his throat—"why was that piece of glass so important?"

It was a very particular question, and it caused a very particular reaction inside Jeremy. He opened his mouth, groping for an answer, but nothing came.

Evan didn't break the silence. Maybe he could feel Jeremy's heart racing through his shirt. Maybe he guessed there was a battle going on.

If he did, he was right, because Jeremy knew if he let the truth out now, everything would change. Five words were pounding in his head, five words that would tip his hand, reveal his secret, break open the glass between him and the world. Five words that might shatter this friendship and wipe away everything he'd gained.

Evan's back moved against his, and Jeremy felt so much fear and yearning well up in him he thought he really might fall. He looked down at the dark waves crashing against the cliff, the spray arcing where it met the rocks. The topmost logs were floating now, battering the stone with each incoming surge.

He wanted to say it. He did. But he was so afraid. Knowing your own secret was one thing, but speaking it, opening your mouth and saying those words to the huge, cold, crashing world, that was dangerous. That could hurt. And there would be no turning back.

Jeremy's chest burned as he sat up, drawing cold air into his lungs. He lifted his chin, feeling all at once that same shifting of boundaries, that stretch he had felt while running, back on the beach under the sunlight.

He spoke his five words into the night.

"Because it was from you."

A star appeared in the darkening sky. The ocean boomed beneath them.

Jeremy's body shook. He had done it. He had broken through.

His brain seemed to foam as adrenaline surged through him. Nothing, not his giddy solo run, not Evan bringing him the magazines, not even their near-death escape, compared to this.

He waited, listening, not daring to turn his head.

Seconds ticked by. The waves crashed, a few late seabirds called, but slowly everything became muffled, lost in Evan's silence.

Jeremy felt him breathing, in, out. In, out.

Fear slipped an arm around Jeremy, chill and heavy. Evan had been quiet before, giving him time to find his answer, but this was different. This silence felt like its own answer.

It was simple panic that made Jeremy half turn, opening his mouth to say something, anything, that might fix the unbearable moment, might let him repair his mistake. But the palm he pressed to the stone at his side met something warm.

He jerked back in surprise. There was a hitch in Evan's breathing, and Jeremy slowly reached out again.

And found Evan's hand.

Evan's hand held out to him. The fingers open.

How long had it been there? How long had it been waiting?

Their palms met. Evan's fingers tangled into his, and Jeremy squeezed, softly, to see if they were real. Evan squeezed back.

There was a long moment, then,

"I like you, too," Evan said.

Nineteen

Jeremy was certain he must have left his body.

"For real?" His voice was a whisper.

Evan ran his thumb along the back of Jeremy's hand. "For real."

Jeremy shivered, and words came tumbling out. "'Cause I like you, Evan. I mean I really like you. A lot."

"Same."

Jeremy couldn't decide if this was the perfect way to be doing this or the worst. He wanted desperately to turn, to meet Evan's eyes, to prove to himself they were both saying what he thought they were saying. But the forced separation was also giving him a confidence he knew he might not have had otherwise.

"I didn't know," he rushed on. "About you. I mean, I couldn't tell. I wished— And there were so many times I wanted to tell you about me. But I was scared of getting it wrong. I didn't want to risk maybe not being friends anymore." He was close to babbling, he knew, but it felt so good to let go. The glass wall, for now, had completely vanished. "Maybe that makes it sound like I was lying or something, but I wasn't! I've just never— And then with you . . . do you know what I mean? Does that make sense?"

"It totally does," said Evan. "I get it. I didn't want to scare you, either."

A sudden crackling boom sounded from somewhere up the beach, then another, and all at once the distant hiss and roar of fireworks blossomed into the night, their echoes reverberating down the cliffs.

The noise startled the flocks of sleeping birds, and hundreds of winged shapes rose crying into the air all along the coastline. Jeremy's seat had him facing north toward Rosemont, and above the sweeping arm of the cliffs he could just make out the tops of a few grand explosions, red and gold and blue, their flashes of rainbow light reflecting off the underbellies of the wheeling birds.

"Okay, um, happy Fourth of July, I guess," Evan said, and Jeremy laughed.

"Happy Fourth of July!"

They listened, their hands still joined, until the celebrations tapered off and the birds settled down, and it was just the two of them again, perched on the side of a cliff out on the edge of the world.

The sea washed in and out. Their hearts beat. The silence between them was full.

"When did you know?" Jeremy asked after a while. "I mean about yourself?"

"Since I was ten," said Evan. "You?"

"For certain? Like, six months ago. Maybe a bit more. Have you, um, told anyone?"

Jeremy felt Evan nod. "I told my cousins and everyone on our fishing trip."

"Wait, a few days ago?"

"Mm-hmm. That was that thing I told you went well. Told my grandma, too, over lunch the day we met you behind the shop."

"Really?"

"I was gonna tell you, yesterday at Lookout Park. But then you brought up girlfriends and stuff, and I chickened out."

Jeremy was flabbergasted. So many signals had gotten crossed. So many opportunities missed.

"I haven't," he said. "Told anyone. Yet."

"I think you might've told me." There was a smile in Evan's voice.

"What made you decide? To tell your family like that?"

Evan let out a long sigh. "I'd been thinking about it for a while. I knew I wanted to do it sometime this summer, before middle school really gets going. Then I met you. Didn't seem any point in waiting."

"Wow," Jeremy whispered. The fireworks had moved inside him.

Evan squeezed his hand. "You think you'll tell your dad?"

The question caught at Jeremy, sending prickles under his arms and around the back of his neck.

"I feel—" he answered, after a long moment. "I feel like I should say yes. Since, you know." He tapped Evan's fingers with his. "But, no, I don't think so. He's— My dad's really different from me, a different kind of guy." Jeremy stared out over his knees, watching the dark water throw itself against the unmoving cliffs. "He thinks life should go a certain way, and he doesn't like when stuff happens outside that. This—this feels like something he wouldn't like. Or at least it would weird him out and make things super awkward between us from now on."

"Makes sense," said Evan. "You shouldn't have to deal with that. What about your mom?"

"She'd be better, I think. Mostly. She's super busy with the move and her new job, but if I told her I like guys, she'd still make it into some big project to tackle. She'd make it, like, *hers*, the way she does with everything else." He stopped, swallowing a laugh. "Man, I'm making my parents sound so weird. It's just— I think I want to keep this part of me mine for now. I don't want to let them in yet."

He felt Evan nodding again. "Totally get that, too," Evan said. "Remember when I told you how running felt like having my own world where I set all the rules? I think that was a major reason why I got into it. I needed that same feeling."

"Smart." Jeremy flicked a flake of moss into the sea. "Part of me still wishes I was as brave as you, though. Even with everything."

Evan made a low, reassuring sound, then straightened and shifted to his left, indicating with his hand that Jeremy should do the same. Jeremy did, feeling his neck curl back into space, and suddenly their heads were resting on each other's shoulders, Evan's cold ear pressed against his, dark hair tickling his cheek.

Jeremy thought he might cry at the tenderness of it: the warmth of the other boy's back, the softness of his hair, the lock of his fingers.

The night and the stars moved on around them, the tide crested and changed, and at last the sea began its retreat inch by steady inch.

Jeremy's mind went fuzzy as the hours slipped by, but his early fear of falling asleep and toppling into the waves never materialized. There was too much of Evan touching him to sleep, too much to think about in their silent conversation. Too much being said in the rise and fall of their slow, grateful breaths.

Staggering to a stop outside the beach house, Jeremy could not have said if returning to it felt more like waking up from a dream or falling back into one. It was somewhere after three in the morning, and the house sat dark and quiet, the bonfire pit with its halo of firework casings abandoned and cold. The party was definitely over.

He and Evan had jogged back after helping each other through a scrambling, tense, and at times terrifying descent from the ledge and the logs. They'd jogged for warmth, mostly, and to stretch the aches out of their cramped legs.

They separated at the gravel driveway, Evan starting off home after a single brief, fierce hug. They were both too tired for more.

Jeremy walked up to the house, worn-out but still floating from his toes to the tips of his cold ears. Cigarette butts peppered the porch, and there were plastic cups and bottles lining the railing, smelling of wine and beer and whiskey. Someone had knocked the remaining white shell from its spot. Jeremy found it and put it back, brushing it clean of the dirt. There were still five full days left. Their second week wasn't over. Not yet.

He let himself in, dimly noticing the mess the kitchen and dining room had become. The living room was better, though there were bottles there, too, and half the sofa's cushions had traveled to the floor. It took almost every muscle fiber left in his legs to sneak his way quietly to the top of the stairs.

His room smelled wonderfully safe and familiar, but when he switched on his light, he spotted a note lying on the blankets beside his phone. It was written on a sheet of notebook paper in thick, drifting permanent marker.

Jeremy—

It's 12:45 and you're not home.
Does that mean you went to Evan's to watch movies? You said you wouldn't.
Hope you enjoyed yourself, because you've seriously disappointed me and your uncle.

I expect an explanation in the morning.
Dad

Shaking his head at his dad's ability to focus on himself, Jeremy blearily scraped up the pieces of an excuse from his exhausted brain. He would have to hope it was enough when day came.

He changed out of his running things and crawled into bed, more grateful for soft sheets and pillows than he'd ever been in his life. Sleep rolled toward him almost instantly, sweeping over the images of Evan behind his eyes, the memory of Evan's hand in his, the soaring freedom of speaking his truths into the night.

Five days left on the coast. Only five days.

And his life had just gotten started.

Twenty

THURSDAY, JULY 5

Jeremy was jolted awake as his attic door banged open with a crash. He rolled over, squinting, to find his dad standing in the doorway, gray bags under his eyes and a frown darkening his face.

"Up, up, up!" his dad hollered, one hand on the doorknob, the other whapping on the wooden frame. "Kids who stay out late don't get to sleep in. Let's go!"

Jeremy sat up, pulling the protective warmth of the blankets with him. He'd been dreaming of crashing waves, and darks rocks, and lightning filling the sky.

"All the way up!" His dad banged the door again for emphasis. "There's cleaning to do, and I want to hear what you thought was so important you could skip out on your uncle's party. Be downstairs in three minutes!"

He left, leaving the door hanging wide. Jeremy listened to his dad stamping down the stairs, then yawned and flopped back on the pillow. It was earlier than he usually got up, judging by the angle of the sun; he'd only gotten a few real hours of sleep. His mom had told him once that sleep was when your mind sorted through all the thoughts and feelings you'd racked up during the day, and if you didn't get enough of it, your brain would go all tangled and muddy. Jeremy suspected it would take a whole month of sleep to sort through the thoughts and feelings he'd racked up over the Fourth.

He shot out a hand to his phone, suddenly excited, but there were no messages since the text from Evan the night before saying he'd successfully snuck back in. The lucky guy must still be sleeping.

Groaning, he heaved himself out of bed, wincing at his sore legs. His dad's words echoed through his mind as he dressed, and resentment crept in to join the sleep fog filling his brain. It wasn't *his* fault he'd missed the party—he and Evan had just made an honest miscalculation about the tide, that was all. There was no way he should be blamed for that.

But he already knew he wouldn't be telling his dad the truth. Even stripping out the most important parts of the story—the feelings he had had on that cliff, the overflowing silence, Evan's hair brushing his neck—his dad would probably find enough to be mad about to give him a heavy lecture on responsibility and respect and smart choices, ruining Jeremy's memory of the cliffs with his own grown-up opinions. Jeremy was not about to risk that, even if it got him in trouble. Last night was his. Only his. His dad had no right to any of it.

Besides, from the shadows under his eyes, his dad had made the most of the party, and Jeremy guessed this wasn't going to be a morning filled with understanding no matter what he said in his defense.

Washing his face and hands had become a habit now, but when Jeremy got downstairs he found the bathroom door closed, the hiss of the shower running behind it. He could see his dad out on the porch, so it had to be Uncle Becker in there. He must have stayed over.

The kitchen in daylight was a disaster of dirty plates, beer bottles, spilled wine, chicken bones, squashed grapes, and the remains of a red-white-and-blue sheet cake, but Jeremy managed to make enough room around the sink to wash his hands and splash water on his eyes. He was drying off with paper towels when his dad came in from the porch.

"So," his dad said, planting himself squarely on the other side of the counter. "What's your big excuse, then?"

Haltingly, Jeremy unfolded the story he'd pieced together the night before, describing a last-minute decision to walk back over the cliffs to try and see the fireworks from above, then a chance encounter with some cool and completely imaginary friends of Evan's. He was vague on every one of the details, but his father accepted the story without question, his face growing steadily cloudier.

He shook his head when Jeremy was done. "Wow." He stepped into the kitchen and pulled a mug from the cupboard. "That's worse than I expected. You really let me down, Jer."

"I'm sorry." Jeremy hoped saying it would get this uncomfortable talk over and done with. "It just sort of happened."

His dad looked down at him, and the anger that had been building on his face shifted into something more complicated.

"Okay, look," his dad said, running a hand through his hair. "I know you're growing up, and you want to hang out with your friends. Trust me, I get that! I used to stay out as late as I could when I was a kid. What's bothering me here is you putting that above your own family. Remember what I said before you went off on your run? This was our first holiday with just the two of us, and I was looking forward to it, you know? Me and you spending time together was part of why your uncle let us stay here in the first place. It's part of why I'm paying for it!"

Jeremy kept his eyes fixed on a fly investigating a peach pit beside him.

"What you did was just disrespectful," his dad continued. "I've given you your freedom here, and I thought I could trust you to show some consideration for your uncle and his friends, not to mention me." He picked up his mug and filled it with coffee, setting the steaming pot back with a clack. "So, you're grounded."

"What?" Jeremy's head snapped up. "For how long?!"

"Until I say. You can hang out near the house, but no wandering into town, and no runs with that Evan kid. You stay here, you do the rest of those chores, and you keep out of trouble." His dad slurped from his mug and sighed. "You know I don't like doing things like this, Jer, but you've really disappointed me."

A tidal wave of recent disappointing things about his dad swept through Jeremy's brain, and he had to bite his tongue to keep from shouting them all out at once. No runs with Evan? No trips into town to see him at the shop? No hanging out? For days, maybe? When their time was almost up? No way. That was not an option.

He heard the shower shut off and winced. He had to try and fix this before Uncle Becker came out. His dad would never back down in front of his brother.

"What if I do all the cleaning up from your party? And dishes and laundry for the rest of our time here, too? Can I not be grounded then? Please? It's totally not fair to cut me off from my friend!"

His father was shaking his head before Jeremy finished. "You're cleaning up anyway, Jeremy," he said, with a deliberate evenhandedness that made the back of Jeremy's neck sear. "And deciding to stay out with your friend instead of participating in a family event was what got you grounded. It only makes sense that you don't get to see him for a while as punishment."

"But it's not fair!" Jeremy was raising his voice. He never did that. "We've only got five—"

The bathroom door opened, and Jeremy stopped, looking around at the same time as his dad.

"Oh, am I interrupting? Sorry."

Sandy was standing there. Sandy from the Grill, wrapped in his dad's bathrobe with their one spare towel coiled around her head. She flashed a broad smile, but it faltered as no one returned it.

She looked at them, and her mouth formed a small O. She nodded, holding up both hands in a gesture of understanding, and slipped away into the downstairs bedroom. The door clicked shut behind her.

The heat of Jeremy's anger turned to ice, cutting off feeling in his chest.

Sandy had stayed over. With his dad. In his dad's room. Overnight.

Across the kitchen, his father was gripping his mug with one hand and picking at a smear on the counter with the other, very obviously not making eye contact with Jeremy. A curdled, smothering embarrassment settled over the room.

Neither of them spoke. Jeremy was too thrown to start arguing again. No matter how nice she'd been at the diner and when he ran into her on the beach, Sandy was basically still a stranger, and his father had brought her into their home, and let her sleep there, and probably made her breakfast right here in their kitchen.

The divorce had only been final for a month now. Less. For all Becker's teasing about the joys of the bachelor life or whatever, Jeremy had never guessed his dad would really dive into it. Not like this. Not so soon.

The silence congealed, becoming a new wall between them, until finally his dad cleared his throat, shifting. Jeremy turned his back and made a big production of digging out bread for toast.

"So, yeah, anyway," his dad said. "You're grounded, and your job for the day is getting this place cleaned up. And that's . . . you know. That's it." He coughed again, set down his mug, and went to join Sandy.

Jeremy ate breakfast alone, leaning against the counter in the wrecked kitchen, staring out the window. He felt unwillingly older. Some piece of his childhood he hadn't even known was still there had just dried up and fallen away.

Outside on the beach, the families and tourists were emerging; dogs ran barking along the sand, little kids swung plastic pails, old couples laid out towels and sunscreen. A few thin clouds floated by above the birds. Jeremy swallowed the last of his toast, added his plate to the pile on the counter, and reluctantly started cleaning up.

He did his best to ignore it, but he could still hear the muffled voices coming from his dad's bedroom, then the whispered conversation as his dad and Sandy emerged into the living room. He raised a hand when Sandy called out a goodbye, her voice bright but uncertain, and waved it once in acknowledgment when his dad announced he was driving her back into town.

The second the door closed, Jeremy dropped the wad of paper towels he was holding and sprinted upstairs. He needed to talk to Evan about being grounded. Now. They had to come up with a plan. There were only five days until he left, and after last night, every minute had become unbelievably precious.

There were still no messages waiting when he reached his phone. That was weird. Was Evan feeling shy suddenly? Or nervous about reaching out? The thought sent a happy squeeze through Jeremy's ribs. It looked like it was his turn to get the ball rolling, his turn to take the leap and go first.

Hey! Hope you're getting to sleep in!

Bad news: I'm grounded for missing the party last night. I'm gonna try and get out of it by tonight though. Hang out later, maybe?

He paused, thumb hovering. He wanted to say more. He wanted to text something that would feel like holding hands, or backs pressed together, or heads resting on shoulders. But how was he supposed to do that? People who liked each other probably sent kisses or something at the end of their texts, but he and Evan hadn't done that yet.

Yet. Jeremy suddenly felt like he'd stepped into the world's hottest sunbeam. He pressed send before he could type anything he would regret, stowed his phone and the piece of turquoise beach glass safely in his pocket, and headed back downstairs. If he got the cleaning done super quickly, there might still be a chance he could change his dad's mind.

It was a slim chance, for sure, but until he heard back from Evan and they came up with a better plan, he was willing to work for whatever hope he could get.

Twenty-One

Jeremy's dad didn't even glance at him when he got back from dropping off Sandy. He disappeared into his bedroom instead, clutching his laptop and a bottle of antacids, slamming the door closed as Jeremy went on cleaning. Jeremy was grateful for that; he'd been worried his dad might want to have some sort of talk. He had enough to think about replaying every moment of the night before and wondering when Evan would wake up and write.

Jeremy hauled trash, washed cups, and scrubbed wine spills off the floor, constantly jumping at phantom buzzes from his phone, but as the morning hours marched steadily into afternoon, there was still no word from Evan.

Not that that stopped Jeremy from texting. It took all his self-control just to keep them brief.

> Hi! Guessing you're at work now. Hope it's okay!

> Getting close to done with the chores from my dad. Gonna ask if I'm still grounded soon. Maybe run tonight?

By five o'clock, Jeremy was in a silent frenzy. The house and beach were back to their usual state, the recycling bin over-flowed with bottles, and three stuffed garbage bags leaned against the wall outside. But he was still grounded. And his phone was still silent.

His dad had made brief appearances every few hours for food and coffee, and as far as Jeremy could tell, his angry hangover seemed to have stuck around well into the afternoon. But by dinner-time his dad was out of his room and back on the beer, and his mood improved. He even made an effort with dinner, fixing them both macaroni and cheese with a side of frozen broccoli and mint chip ice cream for dessert. Jeremy wondered if it was meant as a peace offering.

They'd barely spoken to each other the entire day, and Jeremy—still resentful over all the cleaning, angry at being grounded, and anxious about Evan's silence—was happy to keep it that way. Using under a dozen words, they agreed to eat in front of the TV, and soon a noisy alien movie was doing a decent job covering up their silence. Halfway through the movie his dad got up and returned with a glass of ice and a mostly full bottle of bourbon. A few min-utes after that, Jeremy excused himself and headed down to the beach.

His father didn't seem to notice.

Outside, the sun was sinking into a low bank of clouds rolling in from the west. Jeremy watched it go, kicking at the sand.

Twenty-four hours before, he and Evan had been running with the wind in their lungs and that incredible sense of freedom in the air. Now Jeremy felt like he had wet seaweed wrapped around his chest. He was cold, and the air felt flat. And Evan had still not written back.

He walked down to the waterline, trying to piece together the possible reasons. Maybe Evan was in trouble for staying out and not allowed to use his phone. Or maybe his phone had died somehow. Or their magical personal network had just stopped working.

But no matter what he thought up, Jeremy's brain kept returning to the worst and likeliest reason: that he had misinterpreted everything, that Evan had never meant to hold hands, that he had been freaked out by Jeremy clinging to him all night and was going to avoid him until the clock ran out and Jeremy left and Evan was free of him forever.

The very idea made Jeremy stop breathing, but he couldn't keep his mind away from it. He paced the foam at the edge of the sea, words whispering through his brain—*it's over, you ruined it, it's over, you ruined it*—until the last light faded from the clouding sky.

Chilled, he wandered back to the house, where he found his father snoring in front of the movie's menu screen. He set a glass of water beside him, turned off the glowing set, and climbed the steps to his room, letting the floorboards creak.

Kicking off his shoes, he flicked on the lamp and dropped, fully dressed, across his bed, staring up at the ceiling and letting go of the very last of his hopes.

It didn't even matter anymore, being grounded.

He had ruined things, and Evan was letting him know, and there was nothing to do but lie low, and go back behind his pane of glass, and wait for the whole disastrous trip to be over.

Something sharp clattered against Jeremy's window, and he woke, blinking and groggy, his bedside lamp still glowing beside him. His phone told him it was 10:55. He'd only been asleep for an hour.

He sat up and peered out into the dark, squinting to make his eyes adjust.

A figure was standing in the shadows off the porch, one arm pulled back to throw. Jeremy stared, then started forward without thinking, smacking his face on the cold glass.

White teeth flashed as the figure smiled, switching from a throw to a wave.

Jeremy yanked the window open, pushing his whole upper body directly into the cool, welcoming night.

"Hey!" he called in a hoarse whisper.

"Hey," Evan called back.

Twenty-Two

They had an awkward start. Jeremy assumed Evan would climb up, like before, and Evan seemed certain Jeremy would be coming down. They whisper-shouted simultaneously, speaking over each other, then did it again. Both of them grinned, but alongside the worry they might wake his dad, Jeremy still felt a hollow of hurt in his belly. Evan was here, yes, but what for, exactly?

Seesawing between brave and nervous, he stuffed his feet in his shoes, threw on a jacket, and climbed carefully down, dropping from the railing just in front of Evan.

He stopped, unsure what should happen next, but he didn't get to decide. In the space of three heartbeats, Evan's arms had wrapped around him in a hug, and Jeremy felt his own arms leap into place over Evan's shoulders like they'd never known any other home.

They stood like that for a long minute, holding each other. Evan smelled like shampoo, and his sweatshirt was the softest worn-out cotton. So much relief and joy swept through Jeremy that he thought his legs might give out. He hadn't ruined everything. It was all okay.

Evan started speaking the moment they broke apart, telling Jeremy how he was grounded, and his phone had been confiscated until tomorrow. He'd been worrying all day what Jeremy must think and snuck out the second his grandma was asleep. Jeremy kept waving his hands to make Evan keep his voice down, but the relief in his heart still turned up to fifty as every one of his terrifying theories from before melted away like bad dreams.

"There's something I really want to show you," Evan said, his eyes bright. "Can you come hang out?"

Jeremy looked back at the dark house, where the only light came from his bedside lamp in the attic. He'd never snuck out before, not really. Once when he was seven, he'd climbed out his bedroom window past the rhododendron and tiptoed around the yard, feeling brave and grown-up and incredibly guilty. It had rattled his young mind to realize his parents didn't know, didn't see the truth of it shining out of him at breakfast the next morning. He still remembered his dawning understanding, amid the crunch of toast and cereal, that there were things in his life that he could keep entirely his own, separate and secret and safe.

Jeremy wondered what that younger self would have thought of this moment, five years later, out beyond all the boundaries he had known. He grinned and nodded.

"Yes!" Evan said. He ducked down to pull a backpack from the shadows below the porch. "Supplies so we're not cold this time," he explained at Jeremy's look.

"Oh, so we're heading back to the cliffs?"

"Ha! No, this is better. Come on."

They walked side by side, heading north up the pebble line. The clouds from sunset had rolled in, forming a heavy gray ceiling tinged with orange where it caught the lights of town. The air smelled like salt and something that might have been rain. Most of the other houses were dark, but light spilled from a few windows, sending thin golden rectangles slanting down through the seagrass.

Looking out, Jeremy noticed that the water to their left was only just beginning its climb up the sand. Thanks to the shifting rhythm of the tides, the trap they'd been caught in would be happening almost an hour later tonight. Any night but last night and they wouldn't have been trapped at all. And then maybe neither of them would have said what they'd said. Maybe they would never have held hands.

He wanted to hold hands now. Evan was only a step ahead of him. It would have been the easiest thing in the world to reach out and take one swinging palm in his.

But he couldn't do it. Not here. This wasn't their private cliff perch. There were people in the houses they were passing, and eyes to see them, and as much as Jeremy wanted to feel Evan's fingers wrapped around his, he didn't want the fear of being discovered to spoil it. He wanted the separate, windswept freedom he'd felt last night, the whole world shrinking down to just the two of them, with no one else's opinion there to matter.

After about half a mile Evan changed the angle of their walk, and Jeremy saw they were heading for the driftwood forts he remembered passing on their second run. He also remembered, with a wave of heat prickling his scalp, what Evan had told him about the forts, and teenagers, and nighttime.

But apparently Rosemont's teenagers were all partied out from the night before. There was no firelight shining between the stacked logs, no voices or laughter. They had the forts to themselves.

Evan led the way, making a beeline for a structure set slightly apart from the others.

It looked something like an L-shaped tent, about four feet high, with a sloping roof and a narrow entrance set into the shorter end. The main section branched off to form a chamber ending at a heap of blue-gray stones that might once have been intended for a wall. The whole thing was made of driftwood logs, gnarled branches, sticks, and dried beach grass, all tied in with rope and netting.

For a building made entirely out of scraps, it seemed surprisingly solid.

"So," said Evan, coming to a halt beside it. "This is what I wanted to show you. Welcome to my fort."

Jeremy lifted his head. "*Your* fort?"

"Yup. Someone else started it a long time ago, but they did a terrible job. It kept collapsing and was this sad wreck forever. So, three summers back, I made it my mission to fix it up."

"That's so cool!"

"Thanks. It was, you know, kind of a big deal for me, doing it by myself." Evan patted the side of the structure, a blend of pride and embarrassment in his voice. "I mean, I had some help. I was only nine, and my older cousins were still coming here for the summer then. They took turns saving it for me every day and helping to carry the logs. They even got me some of that yellow *caution* tape

after a bit so I could close it off when we had to go home for dinner."
He smiled. "To be honest, I think they were just happy I was doing
something that kept me from hanging around them all the time. I
could get pretty clingy. Until I finished this place, at least—after
that they practically had to drag me out. I even started calling it my
castle." He glanced up at Jeremy. "Um, anyway, yeah! Hang out here
for a second, then come in when I tell you."

Evan and his bag vanished into the fort. There was scuffling, a
pause, and a soft light appeared around the bend.

"Okay, now you!"

Jeremy crouched down and followed.

Evan was sitting cross-legged in the side chamber, the mound of
rocks at his back, gathering up flecks of trash by the light of an electric camping lantern. Carvings and graffiti covered the inside of the
fort: names and dates and swear words marking every inch of wood,
flickering between the lantern light and the shadows Evan cast as
he moved.

Jeremy hesitated. "Hey," he said, suddenly nervous.

"Hey." Evan patted a patch of sand beside him, and Jeremy scooched
in. He wondered how close he should sit. So close their knees were
touching? Or should he leave a space?

He decided to leave the space. Even though they'd already held
hands and been back-to-back for hours, this wasn't the cliff ledge.
Things were different tonight.

Tonight was on purpose.

"This is so cool," he said again, louder than he'd meant to.

"Thanks." Evan reached for his backpack. "And ta-da! Supplies." He pulled out a small mini-mart in snacks: chips, cookie packs, gummy worms, bottled water, pretzels, and sweet iced tea in cans.

"You didn't have to do all that!" said Jeremy. "Now I feel bad for not bringing anything."

Evan shook his head and opened two teas. The cans were green, with a picture of a flowering cherry tree on them, and Jeremy took a sip. He'd never really tried iced tea, but sitting in this fort beside Evan, it was the best thing he'd ever tasted.

"Thank you," Jeremy said. "For everything." His eyes met Evan's, and they both glanced away. The air prickled.

"You said you were nine when you built this?" Jeremy asked, just to say something. He reached up to push at the ceiling. "I bet I couldn't build something like this now. Did you do the carvings, too?"

Evan huffed a laugh. "Only a few. Lots of people have added to it."

"Well, which ones are yours?"

"That one, and that one, and . . . that one." Evan pointed out a large carving of the letter *E*, a castle drawn in permanent marker, and a detailed carving of a crown.

"Wow, that's really good! Does it ever weird you out that all these strangers come in here and add their own marks?"

"Nope. It's part of the beach. I like people adding carvings, so long as they don't mess up mine. And so long as they don't find the armory."

Jeremy looked over. "Okay, the what?"

Evan smiled, then rose to his knees and turned to the pile of stones. Jeremy watched his shoulders move as he strained, lifting something. There was a scraping, followed by a clang, and when Evan turned around he was holding a rusted metal coffee can. A dark gap yawned in the wall behind him.

"Three years, and no one's ever found it," Evan said. He sat back down, closer to Jeremy this time. Jeremy shifted forward, too, and their knees connected.

For a moment, everything went still, the only sound the rolling waves outside, the only sensation the point of heat where he and Evan met. Jeremy felt like his brain had been blotted out. It was ridiculous; they'd been pressed together for hours the night before. They had held hands. They had said they liked each other. They had hugged! Why was everything still so overwhelming?

"So, um, what's in the can?" he asked, blinking away a tremor in the corners of his eyes.

"Secrets. Big secrets. You have to promise not to tell anyone."

Jeremy raised a hand and promised.

Evan dug his fingers under the black plastic lid, then paused. "And you have to promise not to laugh."

Jeremy laughed. "Sorry, that was the last one. Really, promise."

Evan narrowed his eyes, then opened the can and dumped its contents onto the sand. It took everything Jeremy had to keep his word.

"Dinosaurs?" he said, his voice going squeaky.

"My army, from when I was nine. I left them here to defend the castle."

Jeremy picked up a tiny green triceratops and made it clomp through the air. "I guess they're doing a good job if no one's found them."

"Yup. You, uh . . . you're the only person I've ever shown them to. Figured you're trustworthy."

Jeremy pointed the triceratops at Evan and gave his best roar. It sounded like a Heermann's gull. Evan snatched up a diplodocus and bawled a reply.

And without anyone suggesting it, without planning, and somehow without any embarrassment, they settled down to play dinosaurs. The cans and snack wrappers became an ancient Jurassic swamp, gummy worms rolled in sand became an invading alien army, and soon ranks of dino defenders were charging in to save the day, and both of them were laughing over Jeremy's terrible dinosaur sounds, and the tangled world beyond their circle of lantern light faded away completely.

Twenty-Three

"Hey, remember this time yesterday, when the ocean was trying to kill us?" Evan said.

The dinosaur army had won, and the boys were lying stretched out in the small space, their backs to the rocks. The lantern flickered, and Evan gave it a shake.

"I think I do," said Jeremy. "I like this better, though. More dinosaurs and iced tea. Less chance of drowning."

He'd been watching Evan from the corner of his eye: the angles of his face, the light and shadow playing on his jaw, his eyebrows, his nose. He felt an almost overwhelming urge to reach out and touch Evan's temple, right where that perfect dark hair met his skin.

"Definitely less chance of drowning," Evan said. He turned his head, and at the sight of his eyes the old magnetic tug heaved at Jeremy's heart. He shivered.

"Oh, are you cold?" Evan leaned forward to rummage in his bag, and Jeremy realized with some surprise that, yes, he was cold. The wind had changed, and a knife of ocean chill was slicing through a gap in the logs beside him. Evan returned with a wool blanket patterned with horseshoes. "Here, get under here."

They shoved aside their dinosaur kingdom so Jeremy could scooch closer, and Evan unfurled the blanket. A fair amount of shifting occurred to get them both covered and comfortable, and by the time they settled, their legs and shoulders were pressed close together. Jeremy could smell the iced tea on Evan's breath.

The lantern flickered again, going all the way off. Evan reached out and thumped it, and it came back, but only at a dim half glow, making everything in the fort the color of dark honey.

Jeremy barely noticed. The blanket was very warm. He was very aware of Evan.

He would have given anything to hear what was going on inside Evan's head just then. To know what he should do in the silence. He was nervous, and hoping, and scared.

Evan's leg was trembling. Jeremy felt something building in his chest.

He reached out a hand, amazed at his own daring, and brushed the hair off Evan's forehead. Evan closed his eyes, the trembling spreading to his shoulders, and when he opened them again, he found Jeremy's and didn't look away.

"Hey, let's try this one over here!"

Both boys gave a violent start as the world came shoving back in with shouting outside and the crunch of footsteps in the sand. Jeremy thought in a flash of teenagers, and all his old instincts slammed into place. He tugged away from Evan, kicking frantically at the blanket—

Then froze as a teenage girl crawled inside the fort.

The girl stopped, her eyes going perfectly round at the sight of them. She was sixteen, maybe, with copper-brown skin, curly black hair, and a blanket of her own thrown over one shoulder. Jeremy stared, his panicked brain picturing what she must be seeing: two boys, half-wrapped in a blanket, snack food wrappers and plastic dinosaurs heaped in the sand beside them, their faces full of terror and their legs all tangled. Two boys caught somewhere between childhood and whatever came next.

Two boys absolutely, undeniably, caught.

The girl stared at them for the longest ten seconds of Jeremy's life. He braced himself for all the things he had ever heard or imagined would happen if this moment came, while somewhere at the back of his mind he thought how unfair it was that this was happening in Evan's very own fort. His castle, where, of anywhere on earth, they should have been safe.

But then the girl smiled. Smiled and twisted her head over her shoulder. "Hey, babe?" she called. "Looks like this one's taken. Let's try farther down." She turned back long enough to give Evan and Jeremy a wink and a thumbs-up, then vanished.

They stayed frozen, listening as the girl said something, and another voice—another girl's voice—said something back. The footsteps moved off, fading away into the constant sighing of the waves.

Jeremy blinked, a great many things shifting around in his mind at once. Beside him, Evan let out one of his short, huffing laughs. Jeremy joined him.

They sat together in the honey-gold light, letting their galloping hearts settle.

"So, hey, we should probably . . ." Evan finally said, and Jeremy understood. Whatever moment they'd been in had passed. The outside world had reminded them of its existence. Their night had gone as far as it was going to go.

They returned the dinosaurs to the secret armory, packed up the snacks and wrappers, and made their way out into the darkness. The wind had died down, and a fine misty rain was falling.

"Nice," said Evan, hitching the backpack over his shoulders. He turned his face up to the sky.

"What are you doing?" Jeremy asked.

"I like this kind of rain."

Jeremy watched him, feeling the soft tickle of rain across his own forehead and cheeks, until he couldn't take it anymore and threw his arms around Evan. Evan, laughing, wrapped the blanket around them. The rain made a gray curtain against the world, and after another long, silent stretch of time that Jeremy knew he would carry with him for the rest of his life, they each took a corner of the blanket in one hand, tangled their fingers together in the other, and headed for home.

They were cold by the time they reached the beach house. The blanket was heavy with rain, and Jeremy had to admit the lamplight shining in his bedroom window looked very inviting.

They said good night with one last damp hug. Jeremy looked back as he climbed into his window and saw Evan watching, making sure he got in safe. A raised hand and he was gone, and Jeremy stood, dripping on the hardwood floor, back in his own attic room but a thousand miles away from the place his night had started.

Twenty-Four

FRIDAY, JULY 6

Jeremy came downstairs the next morning, yawning and happy, to find his dad showered, shaved, dressed, and already tapping away at his computer.

He was relieved to see Sandy wasn't around. Neither of them had mentioned her once the day before, and that was just fine with Jeremy. It was awkward enough remembering the encounter; if his dad tried to sit him down and discuss it, possibly going into horrifying details about what it meant to be forty-four and single, Jeremy was certain he would implode from embarrassment. So long as Sandy wasn't making any more sudden appearances, he hoped they'd never have to talk about it, ever. After all, there was nothing wrong with silence and avoidance. They were old, trusted friends.

"Morning," his dad said briskly, looking up as Jeremy walked in. "Listen, with your uncle gone for the next four days, I want you to be sure and finish whatever chores are left before he gets back. Think you can do that?"

Jeremy thought of the list his uncle had taped to the fridge and nodded.

"Good. Also," his dad went on, "I've got two important grant applications due by five this afternoon, so I need things quiet again."

"Sure." Jeremy had a sudden flash of hope. "Can I be ungrounded, then? So I can get out of your way?"

His dad gave his bark-laugh. "Ha! Nice try, but nope. Grounded is grounded. Stick to the house, just quietly."

So Jeremy spent the morning sitting cross-legged on his bed, going through the magazines Evan had given him. It wasn't a bad way to spend the day, and when Evan got his phone back and texts started coming through, it got even better.

Jeremy texted Evan a highlight reel from the magazines, mostly from one of the *Vogues*, which was from the late nineties, when fashion apparently meant wearing sporty crop tops and hip belts covered in rhinestones. Evan replied with descriptions of the customers squeezing through the aisles at Tidepool Knickknacks. Sadly no one had bought the French horn or chain saw yet, so they made up a story about someone rushing in and buying both.

I bet she'd pay for them in gold.

Definitely, or gems

"Here, take this ruby necklace! I must have a French horn and an antique chain saw! The fate of the universe depends on it!"

And no one would ever believe me

> What if you tried on the necklace and disappeared though?

Shoot of course that would happen. Where'd I go?

> Here!

Done

Customer. Gotta go

> Don't put on the necklace!

He returned to the magazines, spreading them out open to his favorite pages.

He was so lost in the pictures and thinking about Evan that he didn't register the squeak of approaching footsteps until it was almost too late. There was barely time to upend his blankets over the magazines before his dad appeared, rapping his knuckles on the doorframe.

"Hey," he said. "I just remembered— Uh, what are you doing?"

Jeremy, standing beside the mess of his bed, forced himself to stop swinging his arms. "Nothing."

His dad's eyes flicked over the scene, his eyebrows angling inward, but to Jeremy's infinite relief, he didn't push. "Just heard from your mom," he continued. "Sounds like you haven't called in a while. She wants you to check in."

"Oh, okay."

"Also, the party wiped out our food, so I'm heading into town for groceries to carry us through till we leave. You can come with me and call her from the car."

"Wait, now?" Jeremy said.

"Somewhere else you need to be?"

"No! I just have to . . . finish . . . something."

His father didn't try to hide the suspicion on his face this time. He eyed the lumpy end of the bed. "You know part of being grounded is not getting into any more trouble, right?"

Jeremy swallowed and nodded. It wasn't trouble that worried him; it was the thought of having to explain the fashion magazines to his dad. There was no way he would understand. He might make fun if he saw them, or joke—or worse, start connecting the dots. He might leap to conclusions about Jeremy's very biggest secret, and then from there about the time he was spending with Evan. One glimpse and he might uncover every last thing that Jeremy was trying to keep private.

"Well, we're leaving in three minutes," his father said finally. Still frowning, he turned and left.

As soon as the stairs stopped squeaking, Jeremy jumped into overdrive, stashing the magazines back under his mattress and hastily remaking the bed. He hurried downstairs to find his dad twirling his keys on the porch.

Two texts from his mom appeared in Jeremy's phone as they pulled into the grocery store parking lot, one from the day before and one from that morning, both asking when he was going to call. He smiled, partly at her crisp, affectionate tone, but mostly at the confirmation that for whatever mysterious reason, phone reception between him and Evan still operated under completely different rules.

"I want you to tell your mom you were grounded, Jer," his father said as he got out of the car. "And the truth about why. She needs to know I'm doing some real parenting out here."

Jeremy hadn't been planning on telling his mom much of anything, but if his dad was proud of his "parenting," it was a sure bet he'd tell her himself at some point anyway. He nodded, then said, "Hey, wait—*were* grounded? Am I not anymore?"

"You are through the rest of today. Starting tomorrow you're free. Tell her that, too." Jeremy fought back an enormous smile. "And, Jer?" His dad pointed through the open window. "I don't want to suspect for one second you might have left this car while I'm gone. You are glued to that seat."

The idea of leaving had never crossed Jeremy's mind, but as he watched his dad walk away, he realized it actually was a real option. They were right in the middle of town; if he ran, he could be at Tidepool Knickknacks in two minutes. He could say hello to Evan, maybe even get a hug, and be back before his dad knew a thing. They were so close.

Then again, it looked like a busy day in Rosemont. Two giant Coastal Tours buses were casting shadows over the far side of the grocery parking lot, and every view out the car windows showed bustling streets. The knickknack shop would probably be busy, and as much as he wanted to see Evan, it wasn't worth the risk of getting grounded for the few days they had left. Not just for a smile and a possible hug.

He stayed put and called his mom.

"Hi, honey!" she said, answering on the first ring. "Oh, it's been too long since we talked! My work started yesterday, as you know, and would you believe it, I've got the entire day today to do one online orientation. I finished it in about an hour, and now I'm just sorting out the best way to set up my office. I can't wait for you to see this place, Jeremy; there are so many opportunities! Oh! And the house! I found a wonderful rug at the farmers' market—I know, rugs at the farmers' market? Who knew?—and I ordered a dresser for your room. You still like blue, right? The color is called terabyte for some strange reason, but I promise it's a really lovely blue with gray undertones."

Jeremy put his feet up on the glove box, lowering the visor to keep the sun off his face.

"We'll have to pick out your new bedding when you're here," his mom continued. "I've done some research and think I've found the best deal in town, though that's not something we need to worry about quite so much anymore. This *job*, Jeremy, I cannot tell you. And this house! I never thought it would feel so good to be able to set up every single thing exactly as I wanted. I should have done this years ago! I—"

She broke off, clearing her throat, apparently realizing what she'd just said.

"And how are you, sweetie?" she asked. "Are you still doing okay? Are you wearing enough sunscreen? How's everything going with your dad?"

It took Jeremy a moment to remember where things had stood the last time they'd talked. It had been his second morning in Rosemont, the day after he and Evan met, before they started running. He raised his eyebrows. Only nine days, but it felt like a lifetime ago.

"I'm good," he said. "Things with Dad are fine. And yeah, I'm wearing plenty of sunscreen." He was stalling, trying to plot out what to share since there was even more he didn't want to say this time.

There were the things he couldn't tell her, of course, like how he'd been sneaking out at night and almost drowned and spent half a night trapped on the side of a cliff.

Then there were the things he didn't want to tell her: Evan's gift of magazines and the hours they spent talking in his room; the driftwood fort, the dinosaurs, and the walk home holding hands; the seabird language that was filling in the little gaps in his life. Those were all part of his private world with Evan, and even though his mom would probably be way more understanding than his dad, he still didn't want to open it up to anyone.

He couldn't keep Evan out of his news completely, though, so he told his mom he'd made friends with a local kid and that they'd been running together. His mom was delighted, especially when he told her about buying the very good pair of running shoes.

"Oh, sweetie, how wonderful!" she said. "That's exactly the sort of thing I hoped you'd spend the money on. I *love* how responsible you're being."

Jeremy couldn't help feeling a little guilty at that, so he jumped into a recap of his day trip with Uncle Becker, which reminded him of his dad and what he'd been asked to say.

He didn't want to give his mom too many details about the night of the Fourth, so he skimmed, focusing on the fact that he'd missed his dad and Becker's party because he was hanging out with his new friend and was grounded until tomorrow because of it.

"Well," his mom said when he was done. "Thank you for telling me, but I have to say I don't understand. I mean, my instinct is to *congratulate* you on finding a way out of a party that probably wasn't appropriate for a twelve-year-old anyway! At least from what I remember about your father and uncle when they get together. Spending time with one of your peers was absolutely more important for your social development, and I'm proud of you for that. It baffles me your dad thought grounding you was an appropriate reaction, but then again, I'm not the parent on-site." She sighed. "This is all very confusing, Jeremy. And I'm sure more for you than anyone else."

Jeremy's phone dinged in his ear, then again, then twice more. He pulled it away to sneak a glance, but the preview only confirmed that he had a stack of new texts. They had to be from Evan.

"You're right, Mom," he said, his pulse quickening. "It sure is confusing. Hey, I gotta go . . ."

He wrapped up the conversation as quickly as he could, promising he would keep using the sunscreen, and drink plenty of water when he was running, and be sure not to leave anything behind when they left.

The moment his mom hung up, Jeremy thumbed open the messages, and the conversation he'd just had evaporated out of his head.

Dude we are BUSY. SO MANY PEOPLE IN TOWN

My grandma says I'm un-grounded tomorrow!

She's being super strict about using my phone at work though so I gotta be careful

Hey I think we should add Cassin's auklet to bird words. Check book?

Jeremy was so impatient to get home he jumped out to help with the groceries the second his dad left the store, sprinting the cart back like his life depended on it.

"You have to pee or something?" his dad asked, buckling up.

"Just . . . super hungry?" Jeremy was almost bouncing in his seat. What would *Cassin's auklet* mean? What word was Evan adding?

As soon as the engine turned off in their driveway, he went vaulting up the porch, through the house, and into his room. He snatched up the bird book and riffled through the pages.

There it was, *Cassin's auklet*: a small gray-and-white shorebird, noted for its displays of affection during early courtship. He scanned the description, and one line launched itself off the page and straight into his pounding heart: *Bonds are formed young, and pairs stay together for life.*

It was like the sun and moon and summer stars had all come down together to wrap their glow around him. He speed-texted Evan.

Yes yes yes to Cassin's auklet. What do you want it to mean?

"Jer!" his dad yelled. "Grounded kids are in charge of bringing in the groceries and putting them away! Those are the rules!"

"Coming!" Jeremy typed out a few more lines before he stumbled downstairs.

> Sorry about the tourists!

> Can't wait to hang out!

His dad had disappeared into his room, leaving the car trunk standing open. Jeremy hauled in the bags and soared around the kitchen, barely aware of what he was shoving into the cupboards, then pounded back up to the attic.

His phone was blinking beside his bed.

There was one text from Evan, and it contained only three words.

> Cassin's auklet = Us

Twenty-Five

The news that he and Evan were both about to be free lit a fire under Jeremy, and he got all the rest of his chores done that same afternoon, pulling on the oversized work gloves to weed around the sides of the house, sponge down the dirty siding, scrape gum from between the boards of the porch, and scrub out the garbage and recycling cans.

He was washing his hands at the kitchen sink when his dad, hunched over the table with only a cold cup of coffee beside him, sat up and closed his laptop with a victorious snap.

"Did you get the grants done or whatever?" Jeremy asked.

"Yes!" His dad raised both fists over his head. "Take that, Oregon State Board of Education!" He stood, scratching and stretching. "And now I'm starving. How about we really go for it with dinner tonight, Jer? What's your favorite food?"

Jeremy's favorite food was lasagna, but they couldn't find the ingredients for that, so his dad made grilled cheese sandwiches and pancakes instead. They ate on the sofa, watching a surprisingly fun travel show about luxury Arctic cruises. When it was over, Jeremy's dad hopped up and said he was going to take a shower, and Jeremy wandered to his bedroom to sprawl out and flip through the bird book, one eye on his phone.

"Hey, Jer?" his dad called up the stairs a while later. "I'm heading out to see some of Becker's friends. You'll be okay on your own for a bit, right?"

Jeremy considered asking if *Becker's friends* was code for *Sandy*, then decided he didn't want to know. Besides, his mind was busy with a wonderful realization: If he was home alone, that might mean Evan could come over.

"I'll be fine!" he called. "Have fun!"

He waited until he heard his dad leave, then ran downstairs to make sure, wrinkling his nose at the smell of cologne. He texted the news to Evan.

> Hey! My dad just went on a date or something! Home alone! Think you can sneak out?

It took ten minutes for Evan to reply. Jeremy spent them pacing the kitchen.

> Sorry, we were eating

> And extra sorry, but no. Grandma still keeping eye on me

> Too big a risk

> Wish I could!

Jeremy stopped pacing, his wild hopes for an early reunion crashing to the floor around him.

It was beyond unfair. He and Evan had only just figured out how much they meant to each other, and with only three days left, their grown-ups were still keeping them apart. The clock was ticking! But it looked like for tonight, there was nothing he could do.

Before he'd met Evan, Jeremy probably would have found an evening alone in the beach house fun and exciting. He would have watched bad TV with the volume up, eaten ice cream out of the carton, and found out how high he could jump on the sofa. He still did all that, of course, especially the ice cream, but he spent the bulk of his time swapping texts with Evan.

They settled into an ebb and flow of jokes and news and stories, occasionally dropping in a word or two in seabird. They were being careful with it now, both aware since the cliffs just how much meaning was built into every coded message.

When his dad got home a few hours later, pink faced and smiling, Jeremy said good night and headed for bed. He sat in his window, watching the stars come out over the Pacific and messaging with Evan until sleep finally came for them both, and they swapped a few reluctant final texts.

> Literally can't keep my eyes open.

Saaaaame

> Thanks for hanging out tonight. As much as we could.

You too!

Just yawned so big I hurt my face

No! Protect your face! I like it!

Ha!

You too

See you tomorrow?

I'm working. This is busy season

I can come by the shop.

Yes! Then yes see you tomorrow!

Perfect! Caspian tern/Cassin's auklet!

Caspian tern/Cassin's auklet

Goodnight!

G'night!

Twenty-Six

SATURDAY, JULY 7

Freshly ungrounded, Jeremy hurled himself into town the next morning and found Rosemont overflowing with people again. There were three giant tour buses looming over the grocery store lot now, and the sidewalks and shops were already noisy with vacationers and families and college kids with surfboards. It was the first Saturday morning in July. High summer had officially begun.

Jeremy wove through it all, crossing his fingers that Tidepool Knickknacks would somehow be empty. After more than twenty-four hours apart from Evan, he was feeling the separation in his skin, and the looming pressure of his upcoming departure was snapping at his heels with every footstep.

Sadly, the knickknack shop turned out to be anything but empty. Bodies filled the tiny aisles, squeezing past each other with polite murmurs and laughter. Gloria, wearing a hot-pink button-down and white capri shorts, had climbed right inside the window display, fishing out a green glass vase for a pair of thirtysomething guys to examine.

Evan stood at the register counting out change. He turned at the sound of the bell, and his face lit up with a smile of such open happiness that Jeremy's eyes pricked with tears.

He edged into the shop, hovering by a shelf of novelty coffee mugs until Evan was free.

"Hi!" he said, stepping forward, totally unable to control his smile.

"Hi," said Evan. He leaned over the counter, and for one wild moment Jeremy thought he was about to be kissed, right there in front of everybody.

"So, my grandma says if she catches me texting at work again, she'll take away my phone for a week," Evan whispered. "But she's in a good mood since we're busy, so we can totally go running and stuff later."

"Yes!" Jeremy whispered back. "What time?"

"After we close. So, six thirty, probably? I'll run by and get you."

"What if I meet you here? I could come up early and help you close if you want."

"Sure! Grandma would probably be fine with that. We can close up, run, then get food after."

"Evan, customers first, please!"

Jeremy looked behind him. Gloria had exited the window display, and the men were waiting to buy their vase. She made a shooing motion, so Jeremy shooed, ducking his head and sharing one last smile with Evan on his way out the door.

Gloria watched him leave, too, and he could have sworn he caught a wink from her over Evan's shoulder. Evan had told him the night before that he'd shared everything about the cliffs with his grandma, which meant she knew just how close the two of them had become. That scared Jeremy, but not quite as much as he would have thought. At least it seemed like Gloria approved.

Out on the street, he had to fight down the urge to literally jump with joy. He and Evan had barely made contact, but it was okay; they had seen each other again, and they had plans. They would be together soon.

Still, he noticed, as he set off down the sidewalk, it was starting to feel like he'd spent half his time on the coast burning away the days until he could hang out with Evan.

He'd gotten his fill of the beach house while he was grounded, so he wandered Rosemont for the rest of the morning instead, drifting happily with the crowds. It felt good knowing the place so well now, like he was a local and all these people were the real outsiders.

When he'd had enough wandering, he bought himself a soda, the same kind he and Evan had shared, and found a shady place to people-watch up in Lookout Park. He tried to keep himself distracted by focusing on the summer fashions walking by, but he couldn't stop checking his phone, even though he knew Evan wouldn't be texting from work anyway, and his stomach knotted with every glimpse of the time. The sun seemed to be crawling across the sky. He almost wished he'd saved some of the chores from the day before, just to keep himself busy.

He was walking back toward the beach, needing food soon and short on money, when he heard a car horn honking. He looked up and spotted his dad stopped under a red light.

"Hey, Jer!" His dad shoved his head and one entire arm out the window, waving unnecessarily. Some of the other waiting drivers turned to look, and Jeremy, mortified, waved a few fingers back.

"What are you up to?" his dad called.

"Um, going home to make lunch."

His dad held a hand to his ear. "Lunch?"

"Yeah!"

"Good! I'm going out for a bit, but we can hang out later, okay?"

The light turned green. His dad stayed put.

"Uh, yeah, okay," said Jeremy. One of the cars waiting behind his dad honked.

"Gonna be a great one, Jer. Our last Saturday night here!"

More cars started honking.

"Sure. Yeah. See you later." Jeremy was too embarrassed to know what he was saying. He waved again, taking a few steps so his dad would understand he wanted to leave. His dad gave a thumbs-up, honked his own horn at the growing noise and shouts, and zoomed away into town.

His face searing, Jeremy put his head down and hurried on toward the beach, summoning up happy thoughts of all his plans with Evan, pushing the encounter with his awkward father firmly to the back of his mind.

Twenty-Seven

Jeremy spent the hours after lunch beachcombing near the big log where he and Evan used to meet. He didn't find much beyond a rusted bike chain, a green rock with a hole in it, and a few pieces of clear beach glass, but it filled the time well.

When he got back to the house, his dad was out front, watching baseball on his laptop with a contented smile across his face. "Havin' a great day, Jer?" he asked, rocking back in his chair and raising a bottle of Mason's.

Jeremy nodded, giving half a smile of his own in return, grateful if a little confused that his dad's good mood seemed to be sticking around. He slipped past, heading up to his room.

His dad came inside a while later, clattering around the downstairs and—for some reason—whistling. Jeremy refused to investigate. All he wanted to do was lie on his floor and savor the anticipation of the upcoming evening.

The feeling increased when his phone dinged beside him, announcing back-to-back texts from Evan.

I'm allowed to send this one!

Grandma says she'll take us out for pizza after run

Sound good?

Jeremy had never typed the word *YES* so fast in his life.

He jogged downstairs at a quarter to six to find his dad in the kitchen, wearing an apron again and surrounded by an almighty mess. Water splashed from a giant pot boiling over on the stove; grated cheese spilled out of a family-sized baking dish; and spinach, sausage, peppers, and tomatoes were lying everywhere in various stages of being diced, chopped, and smashed. Jeremy barely glanced at any of it.

"See you later," he called, heading for the open door.

"Hey, hey, hey!" His dad turned, waving a wooden spoon. "Where do you think you're going?"

Jeremy spotted a half-finished bottle of red wine on the counter. Surf-guitar music burbled out of the radio.

"Um, running with Evan."

"Again?" His dad heaved a theatrical sigh. "Well, don't be long. Dinner will be ready in about forty-five, give or take."

"Dinner?" Jeremy shot a look out to the world beyond the porch; freedom was so close. "I'm eating with Evan tonight. After the run. His grandma's taking us out for pizza."

The smile on his dad's face buckled.

"What are you talking about?" he said. "We had plans. We agreed when I saw you on the street."

Jeremy tried to remember one single word about dinner in their exchange, but could only come up with honking. "I don't—I didn't get that, I guess."

"Huh. Well, okay, then surprise! We had such a good time last night I thought we should do it again. See? I'm making lasagna!" The smile was back as his dad waved a hand at the bubbling pot and the baking dish waiting on the counter. "I looked up a recipe online and went into town special and everything. We gotta celebrate; it's our last Saturday on the coast!"

"I know, you said," said Jeremy. "That's part of why I'm hanging out with—with my friend. And his grandma's offering to pay, so—"

"So, you can thank her and cancel."

"I already said yes." Jeremy took a sideways step toward the door. "And I promised I'd get there early and help close the shop."

"Oh, you promised you'd help close the shop?" His dad's mouth tightened, and he crossed his arms, nodding. "Well, don't let me keep you, then, since these people are so much more important to you."

"Dad, come on. I've been grounded. We haven't been able to hang out."

"And whose fault was that?"

Jeremy clenched his teeth to stop himself from answering.

"You know, I can't believe this, Jeremy," his dad said. "I do all this work—I even picked up a present today! Something cool for us to share!

"That's great. Thanks. For everything."

"I just—I thought we'd . . . I don't know, had a breakthrough, or something."

Jeremy had been working his way toward the door, but he stopped as he and his dad stared at each other. The wind off the beach tugged at his T-shirt.

His dad hunched his shoulders, spreading his hands flat on the counter like he was trying to keep the house fixed in place and Jeremy along with it. The expression on his face was complicated, a mixture of disappointment, frustration, and, plainly, hurt.

Jeremy thought he could maybe understand why. Apparently his dad had done all this as a sort of father-son gesture. He'd made an effort, as well as he could, and had been expecting a different kind of result. Jeremy could see that.

But just then he couldn't entirely care.

It wasn't his fault his dad had gone to all this trouble. He'd never asked him to. And Evan was waiting. Evan and everything they'd built between them were finally back within reach, and the clock was ticking. His dad would still be around after the coast; they would have years together, one way or another. But these might be the only days he would ever get to spend with Evan.

His father sighed. "It's your choice, Jer," he said at last, raising his hands in surrender.

The boiling pot bubbled and hissed. Jeremy drew a deep breath.

"Sorry, but I'm . . . gonna go."

With a nod, he turned and walked out the door. He was already running as his feet reached the dirt, grateful with every footfall for the growing distance between himself and the mess he was leaving behind.

Twenty-Eight

SUNDAY, JULY 8

Jeremy was surprised to find himself all alone when he came down to breakfast on Sunday. His dad's room was empty, the bed unmade, and the bathroom door stood open. The chairs sat unoccupied on the porch. The car was still there, but he couldn't see his dad out on the beach or wandering among the morning walkers.

He hadn't seen him at all since their misunderstanding the evening before. Or maybe the better word was *argument*.

Jeremy had had a wonderful night once he left, running to the tide pools and back with Evan, then walking out with Gloria to feast on the best pizza of Jeremy's life at a local hot spot. The owner was a friend of Gloria's, and they'd all gotten free ice cream after, every bowl drowning in sprinkles and, for some reason, gummy bears.

For Jeremy, though, the greatest part of his evening had been hauling out the trash when he helped close up the knickknack shop. The cans were in the street out back, and Evan had come along, and the two of them had stolen five whole happy minutes holding hands and reminiscing right where Evan had first given Jeremy his number.

Jeremy had arrived home after nine, full and happy, almost forgetting the tense standoff when he'd left. The kitchen, to his surprise, was back to normal, with no sign of the chaos of earlier, but when he looked in the fridge for a soda, there was no sign of any lasagna, either. It was as if his dad's grand gesture had never happened. All the evidence had been destroyed.

His dad's door had been closed, a movie blaring from the laptop inside, and Jeremy decided he was in too good a mood to knock and say good night, or offer an apology, or really deal with his dad at all. He was still too caught up in Evan world, and his marvelous night.

Now, in the quiet of the morning, Jeremy made his toast and cereal and ate, putting the radio on for company. He searched the house afterward, looking for a possible note or message, but there was nothing.

At last, showered, dressed, and getting worried, he headed out to the beach to search.

He found his dad a few minutes north, standing with his back to the ocean. He had his aviator sunglasses on and was holding a bulky device in his hands, staring up at the sky.

"Hey, morning," Jeremy said uncertainly, coming to a stop a few feet away.

"Morning." His father did not look over but lowered his gaze to the device in his hand, fiddling with the buttons. Up close, Jeremy saw it was a solid-looking remote control. His father's phone was clipped into the top, forming a viewscreen.

"What's that?" he asked.

His father stayed silent for a long moment, then: "Remember how I told you I got us a present?"

". . . Yeah?"

"This is it. It's a drone. A pretty cheap one, but still, I thought we could share it. Only you don't seem to want to share much with me lately, so I figured I'd give it a try myself."

"Oh." The wind whuffled in Jeremy's ears. An intense prickling settled over his scalp and back. A drone wasn't Jeremy's kind of thing at all, but it sounded like his dad had been trying, at least. And without meaning to, Jeremy had really disappointed him.

"So, um, how's it working?" Jeremy asked, wondering if he should say thank you.

"It's okay."

Jeremy looked up into the sky, misjudged the height of the drone, and got a direct eyeful of sun. He ducked, blinking at the afterimage.

"I thought about grounding you again after last night, Jer," his dad said, still watching his phone. "Only, in the end I decided it wouldn't be fair. You didn't actually break any rules. But you really let me down, man. I feel like you're pushing me away a lot these days."

Jeremy felt his stomach go sour. His dad never brought up his feelings like this, and there was a hard edge to his voice that Jeremy didn't recognize. Bitterness. Almost anger.

"I mean, I get that you like hanging out with your new friend," his dad continued. "Believe me, I'm missing Becker here. But I don't see how some kid you met last week could be that important to you. So, what's the deal?" He finally turned to Jeremy. "Have you decided you're done with me? I know I'm supposed to give you until the end of summer to choose and all that, but I get the feeling you already know. If you want to go live with your mom, you can say it. I'll be okay. I just want the truth."

Jeremy stood looking up at his father, trying to remember to breathe. A pair of toast-colored corgis ran by chasing a tennis ball, their tongues lolling out and unthinking joy written across their faces.

He realized right then that everything would've been so much easier if only he were different. If it had been a girl he'd been feeling so much for, he could have just said, and his dad would have understood. He probably would have insisted Jeremy spend every remaining moment of their trip hanging out with her, even.

But it wasn't a girl Jeremy liked, it was a boy, and since Jeremy wasn't ready to have *that* conversation, everything became complicated by his absolutely necessary silence. That silence made things hard. Especially when his dad got his feelings hurt by assuming all Jeremy's decisions must be about him.

"I don't know who I want to live with yet," Jeremy said when he could speak again. His instincts were telling him to give a nonanswer, to stall, to get away from this direct attention while there was still time. "I mean, I have to visit Mom and stuff first, and see the school there, and . . . yeah, I still don't know. Really. Sorry if I made you feel bad, though. It was nice of you to get the drone."

It was the best he could do.

"Okay," his dad said slowly. He sounded calmer, if not exactly satisfied. "I guess that's fair. And yeah, thanks." He took the remote in one hand, rubbing his forehead with the other. "I just wish we could share things again, Jer. It's been a long time since I felt like you and me were on the same— Oh, hell!"

He had fumbled the controller. He grabbed at it, smashing buttons, and the whole setup slipped through his fingers into the sand. There was a metallic whine from above, and they both looked up to see a small silver shape fall drunkenly out of the sky straight into a cluster of seaweed-covered rocks.

"Damn it!" Jeremy's dad shouted. He scooped up the controller, wrenched his phone out of the top, and strode off toward the crash site, cursing. Jeremy followed.

They found the drone upside down, clearly broken. Two of the propellor arms were bent, one was snapped, and the fourth was missing. The casing protecting the camera lens was cracked.

Worst of all—for Jeremy, at least—the drone had landed barely a foot from the body of a dead seabird. He thought it might have been a western gull, from its beak and the remaining tufts of feathers. It lay on its back, neck twisted, wings bent at impossible angles, most of its body already gone, a scattering of yellow bones visible in the sand.

He stared at it, feeling sick.

"Well," his dad said, bending to pick up the drone. "That was a total waste."

The words thudded in Jeremy's gut.

"Could we, I don't know, repair it?" he asked, looking away from the bird, feeling a sudden need to make some sort of offer. "Together, maybe?"

His dad gave a hollow laugh and folded one of the mangled pro-pellor blades, bending it until it snapped in two.

"Nah, it's done. Go on home or whatever you want." He grunted. "You're probably running later, right?"

Jeremy swallowed. "Evan and I were gonna go around six. It's almost our last chance."

His father eyed the wrecked machine. "Well, see you later, then."

"Sorry the drone, you know . . ." said Jeremy. "Also, um, thanks."

He backed away, then turned and headed for the house, his head pounding from the conversation and the afterimage of the sun.

Everything felt strange when he got back. He drank two glasses of water, carried a third to his room, and folded up on his bed, gazing out at the beach and muddling through what had just happened.

How could things be going so well and at the same time so badly?

The memory of their arrival swam over him, and his first view out this window. All he'd hoped for then was safety, to keep to himself, to go on hiding secrets in the unfamiliar setting.

But he'd taken a risk, stepped out into the sunlight for Evan.

He sighed, his breath fogging the ripples in the glass, warping the waves and the high, floating clouds.

Things were far from perfect, but the risk had made him happy. That was something to hold on to.

He wanted more than safety now. He couldn't let himself forget.

Twenty-Nine

Jeremy's dad returned home half an hour after him, slamming the porch door as he came inside. Jeremy stayed up in his room the rest of the morning, sending texts to Evan and flipping through his magazines for the third time, only venturing down when he heard his dad's car driving off. It was past noon, and he was very hungry.

There was a note from his dad on the kitchen counter, a brief scrawl about running out to Target to try and get a refund for the drone, and Jeremy, relieved, was able to eat his lunch on the porch in peace. He climbed back to his room after, a little too full, and promptly fell asleep on top of his covers.

The sun woke him hours later, angling through the window.

It was nearing six, according to his phone, so he changed, still feeling foggy-brained and muzzy as he climbed into his running gear. It had been the weirdest day, but his headache was gone, and he would be with Evan soon.

He was so close to being happy.

His dad was back when he got downstairs, camped out at the dining table watching baseball on his laptop. The beer was back, too—a bottle in one hand, another, empty, sitting by his elbow, dangerously close to the edge.

"Heading out for your run, Jer?" his dad asked, over the sound of the game. Jeremy nodded. "Man, I never would have read you for the running type. But I'm glad, really! Could come in handy once you get to high school."

"Uh-huh."

Jeremy went to the sink, filling himself a glass of water as his dad whooped at something happening on the screen. Jeremy blinked, surprised and a little unnerved that his dad's mood seemed to have flipped so completely since the morning. Maybe he'd decided Jeremy hadn't been letting him down, after all. Or maybe he'd decided to just act like their awkward conversation had never happened.

The second one seemed more likely. The beer was probably helping, too.

An echo of his mom's voice danced across his mind, and Jeremy crossed to the table to retrieve the precarious empty bottle, carrying it back to the recycling bin.

"Thanks," his dad said, watching him. He sat up. "Well, hope you two have fun. And, hey." He waggled his beer. "Bring me another of these before you go, would ya?"

Outside, the beach was nearly as crowded as it had been on the Fourth, smothered in umbrellas and towels and ringing with the screams of kids, the shouts of parents, the blare of music from portable speakers. It was all background to Jeremy. He jogged in place and did some stretching, then waited on the railing until he spotted Evan's flare of dark hair. Even from a distance, he could see Evan was already grinning. Jeremy waved, doing the same.

Evan had almost reached him, and Jeremy was hopping down to the dirt, when the porch door opened and his dad stepped out into the evening.

"Hold up, Jer. I want to say hello to this friend who's been getting all your time!"

Nothing in Jeremy's life had ever felt so precisely like a cloud blocking out the sun.

He froze, panicking, then forced himself to relax. His dad and Evan had met before, and with a few beers in him, his dad would probably just say something embarrassing or tell a story about back when he was their age. So long as he and Evan nodded when they were supposed to, his dad would eventually wave the bottle in his hand and send them on their way. Everything would be fine.

Evan arrived, the smile dropping from his face. "Oh, hey, Mr. Ryden."

Jeremy's dad strode down the steps, his palm out, clearly oblivious to the impact he was having. "Wanted to thank you," he boomed, shaking Evan's hand. "You've been a good influence on my boy with all this exercise. You're keeping him out of the house a lot, though!"

Evan gave a polite laugh. "I guess so."

"Dad, we gotta go," Jeremy said.

"I know, I know, you can't wait to leave your old man all on his own. Hey!" His dad pointed one of the fingers wrapped around his beer at Evan. "You eaten yet?"

"Um, no," said Evan. "We were gonna run first."

"So, no one's eaten!" Jeremy's dad smiled around the porch. "Tell you what, new plan: Skip the run, and I'll take you both out to the Grill. We haven't done dinner there yet, Jer."

The boys turned to each other. Evan twisted a corner of his mouth in a question, and Jeremy gave a tiny shake of his head. All he wanted was for the two of them to be alone. Sitting at the Grill with his father, probably dealing with whatever grown-up weirdness was still going on with Sandy, was at the very bottom of his list.

"Thanks," Jeremy said, doing his best to sound like he meant it. "Really! But maybe another night? Or, like, a lunch or something?"

"Might not be another chance, Jer. We've only got tonight and tomorrow left! No." His dad held up a hand, expansive and beaming. "You bailed on me last night to get pizza with Evan's grandma or whoever; it's only fair I get a turn. Lemme get my shoes and I'll drive us in." He moved to the door, and Jeremy took a quick step after him.

"Hey, Dad, are you—are you sure you should be driving?"

His father's smile flickered out, replaced by a hard flash of anger. "I am *fine*. Son."

Jeremy felt like he'd been shoved.

"But since you mention it—" His dad hitched his smile back on. "Why don't we walk? You're always walking into town, Jer, and it's looking like a perfect night. Yeah, we'll walk. Just give me a minute to get ready."

He vanished into the house, and Jeremy turned to Evan, his heart pounding.

"I'm so sorry," he said, pitching his voice low. "I guess he's been lonely or something since my uncle left, and he told me he thinks I've been avoiding him . . ." He remembered the night before, and the drone that morning, and the hurt in his father's face.

"Could we just take off and run anyway?" asked Evan. "We could be gone before he gets back."

Jeremy shook his head. "That's basically what I did last night, so it would definitely make things worse. He'd ground me until we leave, and we'd never get to hang out again."

Evan brushed a thumb across the back of Jeremy's hand. "I don't want that."

"Me either!" said Jeremy, through his shivers. "So, I think we gotta do this. I'm really sorry."

"Hey, at least we'll be together. And I like the food at the Grill. Maybe it'll be okay."

Jeremy chewed his lip. "Yeah, maybe."

They moved away from each other just as the door opened. Jeremy's dad had put on a dress shirt and combed his hair. He flashed them a winning smile.

"Ready for a guys' night out, boys?" he said. "Let's make this an evening to remember!"

Thirty

Sandy's Grill was packed when the three of them arrived, and the size of the crowd milling inside the door gave Jeremy a sudden flicker of hope. His dad had never been a fan of waiting.

"Um, Dad, maybe we should try some other night? It looks like there's a bunch of people ahead of us."

"I got this, Jer!" his dad replied, walking confidently out among the tables. Jeremy spotted Sandy, a notepad in hand, just before his dad reached her. They spoke, and Sandy laughed, putting a hand on his arm. They strolled back to the door together.

"Well, hello, boys," Sandy said as she reached Jeremy and Evan. "Table for three coming right up."

"Miss, excuse me, we've been waiting!" objected a pink-faced business-man. "We were here first!"

"These gentlemen have a reservation," said Sandy, her smile show-ing all her teeth. She winked at Jeremy, pulled three menus from the greeter station, and escorted them across the red-and-yellow carpet to a booth in the back of the restaurant.

"Thanks, babe," Jeremy's dad said, sliding a hand across Sandy's waist as he dropped into the left-hand seat. Sandy laughed and shushed him.

Jeremy scooched onto the seat opposite, his throat tightening as Evan, following, left a careful gap between them.

"So, what can I get you boys to drink?" Sandy asked, beaming at each of them. Her eyebrows bounced when she got to Jeremy, and he wondered if she was trying to make up for the awkwardness of the other morning. He hadn't seen her since, and although he liked Sandy, he truly just wanted to forget the entire encounter. He hadn't even mentioned it to Evan. Sandy staying the night was part of his dad's weird, grown-up world, not his and Evan's, and the further he could keep those worlds apart the better.

Although, from the way the evening was going, any distance he'd managed to create might be about to vanish.

"Beer and a shot of whiskey for me," said Jeremy's dad. "And, what, Cokes for you two?"

Evan nodded. "That's great, thank you."

"Do you have iced tea?" asked Jeremy. If he was going to be stuck sitting through this dinner, he was at least going to get a drink that reminded him of being happy.

"*Iced tea?*" His father made a noise. "Since when do you drink iced tea?"

Jeremy shrugged. Sandy's smile turned apologetic. "I'm sorry, honey, but we completely sold out over brunch, and I haven't had a single minute to run and buy more. I think we do have some herbal teas, though. Can I get you one of those?"

"No, Coke's fine."

"No, *thank you*," corrected his father. Sandy whapped him playfully with her notepad.

"No, thank you," Jeremy said quietly.

Evan, watching the exchange, pressed his foot against Jeremy's under the table.

"Two Cokes, a beer, and a whiskey," said Sandy. "Coming right up!"

A strained silence settled over them as she left. The chatter of the dinner crowd filled the air, along with the clinking of knives and the rich smell of grilling meat, but Jeremy was too on edge to try talking yet. He could tell Evan was feeling the same. They weren't protected here; they weren't safe. This was his dad's territory, with them dragged along for the ride.

Luckily, Jeremy's father didn't seem to notice. He was clearly delighted with himself for jumping the line and the VIP treatment he was receiving from Sandy, and he hummed contentedly while they all studied their menus. Jeremy kept his head down, reading every item over again even after he'd decided.

Sandy returned with their drinks, giving Jeremy's dad a pinch when he downed his whiskey in one go, then left again with their food orders. Jeremy's dad followed the whiskey with a long slurp of beer, burped, and stretched out on his seat, his feet up on the vinyl, one arm propped behind his head.

"So, Evan," he said, with a bit more volume than was necessary. "How do you like living in this nowhere town?"

Jeremy flinched, but Evan seemed okay answering the question. He talked about living in Newport the rest of the year and helping out at the shop in Rosemont during the summer, explaining how most of his cousins had done the same before him. Jeremy's dad grunted when Evan mentioned the annual fishing trip, and interrupted with a story of his own about how he almost went to work on an Alaskan fishing boat his first summer after college. Jeremy drank his Coke, emptying it too quickly, grateful to Evan for filling in all the "Yeah?" and "Cool" responses his dad clearly wanted.

Sandy stopped by a few minutes later to ask if Jeremy wanted a refill, and his dad decided he might as well order another whiskey and beer while she was there.

Evan, apparently okay talking now that Jeremy's dad had broken the ice, tried to start a new conversation about the different training styles for cross-country and track. For some reason, though, Jeremy's dad seemed less interested in talking about his high school years than before.

"Eh," he said, scratching his chest and waving a dismissive hand after barely a minute. "There's a lot of stuff you get into when you're young that never really works out. No point rehashing it over and over and wishing you'd done things differently." He turned his head. "You've been pretty darn quiet over there, Jer. How about joining the conversation by telling us what's new with you?"

Jeremy, who'd been focusing on Evan's foot against his, jumped and tried to look attentive. He opened his mouth to answer the question, his mind a complete blank . . . and was saved by the arrival of their refills and food.

"Will you tell me about your job, Mr. Ryden?" Evan asked, lobbing out a new subject the moment they all began eating.

Jeremy's father's face lit up.

Under the table, Jeremy tapped Evan's foot twice, hoping Evan understood that it meant *thank you*. His dad was always ready to talk about his work, and tonight was no exception as he drained half his latest beer and launched into an enthusiastic rant about how hard teaching college was, with regular digressions to point out how easy Becker had it being self-employed.

The rant went on for a while, and Jeremy, saved from the spotlight, was grateful for that. But somewhere in the long list of complaints and boasting, while French fries disappeared and glasses emptied, he realized that the beers from home had joined forces with the drinks from the Grill, and his father was becoming truly and properly drunk.

"It's not like he's got a boss to answer to," his father was saying, the words thick around a wad of meat and bun. "Or meetings to sit through or coworkers constantly, you know, *stealing* his *lunch* from the employee fridge. He's not dealing with any—any of that!" He glanced up. "Something wrong, Jer?"

Jeremy, his own mouth full of fried fish, shook his head.

"Then how's your food?"

Jeremy nodded until he could swallow. "It's good."

"Wow! He speaks! What a contrin—contribution." His dad sucked at the beer in his glass. "It's like you're giving me the silent treatment on top of everything else! Come on, tonight's supposed to be a celebration! You can't still be sad about the drone. Look at me! I've already forgotten about—all about it." He laughed, but it was not a happy sound.

Jeremy shifted his eyes to a seam in the vinyl above his father's shoulder, feeling pressure build in his cheeks and the back of his neck. Everything was okay. His dad probably just wanted to blow off steam. It would be over soon, the dinner would end, and he could get back to being with Evan.

"You know, Jeremy," his dad continued. "I really wanted you to take advantage of the opportunity we got here this summer. I mean, it's over now, right? And what have you done? No, seriously, what have you done? Sure, you did some exercise, and okay, that's great. But Jer—Jeremy, I just don't see you *growing*! Like, come on, buddy. Come on, man! Maybe you don't like the reason we're here—trust me, *I* don't. If anyone's got a right to be mad, it's *me*. But it's summer, and we're at the beach, and that makes it the good times. And, Jer, you've got to get the *most* out of the good times while you've got 'em! Aren't I right, Ev?"

Evan's short nod was apparently enough.

"Thank you! This guy gets it! You got to squeeze everything you *can* out of these days, because the good times? Hey, Jer, Ev-man, come on, this is important." He beckoned them in, hunching over his plate. "Good times? The best times? The most important times of your life? They disappear on you. Without one single bit of warning. None. Boom!"

His eyes had turned a watery pink at the corners. They roved between the boys, but for all their staring, they were clearly not taking any information back in. If they had, Jeremy's dad would have noticed the way his son cringed each time he slapped the table to emphasize a word, or the line settling across Evan's forehead, or the glances from other tables as his ranting grew louder.

The tipping point came when, gesturing wildly, Jeremy's dad finally sent his beer glass flying off the table. Glass shattered across the red-and-yellow carpet, and Jeremy heard gasps. Face after face turned their way. His dad threw back his head and laughed.

He laughed for a full ten seconds, his face red, eyes squeezed tight. "No, no," he said when he could speak again, "'s fine, 's fine, it was empty. I finished."

A busser hurried up with a dustpan and broom, but Jeremy's father lurched out of the booth and waved her away. "Nope, no, no, nope! I've got this. Thank you. I'm the repons'ple adult here." The girl backed off immediately. Jeremy's father was tall, and he was drunk, and there was glass crunching under his shoes. A thick silence spread throughout the Grill.

Jeremy's dad squatted down, steadying himself against the table, and began gathering up the bigger shards. He didn't seem to notice his audience. He picked each piece up carefully, pinching with a finger and thumb, plinking them down in a pile. Jeremy wondered what would happen when he inevitably cut himself.

Then Sandy was there, sweeping through the tables, her jaw set. Jeremy's father blinked as he spotted her shoes. He tilted his head back, looking up, and Sandy crouched down just in time to grab his elbows before he tipped over.

"Hey, baby," she said in a low voice. "Thank you so much, but I've got it from here. Why don't you go ahead and finish your food?"

"Baby!" Jeremy's father did not speak in a low voice. "Hey, Jer'my!" he called. "Jer'my! See? Sometimes things are good, then they go bad 'cause you break your drink, but then can—then they can go good again. Sometimes"—he made a kissing face at Sandy—"a beautiful woman comes along and—"

"Okay," Sandy interrupted. "I think it's time for you to go." She stood, attempting to pull him with her.

From one second to the next, Jeremy's father changed. He shook Sandy off and lurched to his feet, angry and tall again. "No!" he yelled. "S'enough! I'm perfec'ly fine!"

Jeremy had yanked his foot from Evan's the moment his dad crouched down, terrified of discovery. Now he reclaimed it, hooking ankle over ankle as Evan pressed back, both of them sharing the only comfort they could amid the unfolding disaster.

"Mike, please sit down!" Sandy was yelling, too, now. "You need to get yourself together!"

"Why?!" Jeremy's father reeled back several paces, swaying like someone aboard a ship trapped in a storm. "Why should I get together? Why should I sit down?" His words were blurring at the edges. "I am just say-ing to my son about what happens—what happens for good and bad things—things in life."

Evan turned in his seat, and Jeremy leaned in to hear him whisper, "Do you think we should call your uncle?"

Jeremy shook his head, breathing back, "He's out of town," and wishing it wasn't true.

His father looked over just in time to catch him.

"But my *son* is not list'ning to me," he shouted, taking two more backward steps as the boys pulled apart. "My *son* is talking t' the friend, who is Evan. And Evan is the one who made my son not be home this trip. The whole point"—he waved his arms—"the whole point was to father-son some time. You know? Bond, like me and Becker! Only he met this kid." A finger pointed mostly in Evan's direction. "And now who is my son? Huh? Who is he? He goes out every day and goes run-ning. Long runs on the beach. Ha! And he drinks iced tea now, did ya hear? Iced tea!" The finger stabbed the air at each word, and Jeremy felt them strike his heart like blows.

Panic burned under his skin. His dad was as drunk as he'd ever seen him, and the whole restaurant seemed powerless to stop him, to interrupt, to end it. His dad's anger blanketed the room, locking them all in place.

"And get this, he also reads fashion magan-zines! Yup! Keeps 'em under his mattress. I looked! My twelve-year-old son'd rather sit up in his room and read about dresses for models than hang out with his old man dad. I mean—what happened? You think you know your— your family, right? You think you know your family, and your son, and then they go an' *change* on you! Always! Jer and me, we get here together and we're cool, cool dad, cool son, and then he meets the friend and wham"—his fist cracked against the closest table—"he turns into a total—"

"Stop."

The word, sharp as a popped balloon, cut through the furious rambling. Jeremy felt his foot slip free, and the whole room turned to look as Evan rose out of the booth.

"What?" said Jeremy's dad, squinting. "What'd you say?"

"I said stop, Mr. Ryden. Please. What you're doing is hurting Jeremy. It's not okay." Evan's voice was quiet but strong. No one else seemed able to make a sound. Sandy pressed a hand to her mouth.

Piece by piece, muscle by muscle, Jeremy's father's handsome, drunken face shifted, his expression becoming truly nasty. He seemed to be inflating, and then the words came pouring out.

"Who the *hell* do you think you are, kid? Huh? Speaking to me about *my* son?! I'm not—I am not hurting anyone! I'm his father! His father! What makes you think get— You get a say?"

It went on, rising in heat and volume, while Evan stood quietly, his hands at his sides, watching Jeremy's father rage.

Jeremy sat alone in the corner of the booth, drowning.

The panic had swallowed him, pressing him into the wall and smothering his brain, forcing him to stay quiet and frozen and grateful for his safety. But he could still feel his heart, and it hurt. That was Evan standing all alone out there. His Evan. His *cormorant* friend. His *Cassin's auklet*.

At last, straining against his dread, he found the spark of anger that had been with him since that very first morning of the trip. He grabbed at it and kicked out as hard as he could, battling the familiar army of voices screaming at him to stay down, stay hidden, stay behind the glass and never let anyone see you, until his head broke the surface and he pulled in one huge, shivering breath.

He looked out into the crowded room. The servers and bussers were clustered, whispering, near the front; Sandy, her pretty face a knot of unhappiness, stood alone and stranded among her guests; table after table of diners stared at his dad, appalled. The whole Grill was watching, waiting for someone to end this. And none of them could. None of them knew how to reach the man behind the anger.

Jeremy slid slowly across the creaking vinyl and eased himself out of the booth. Broken glass crunched as he found his feet.

He took a step toward his father.

He almost felt as if he were actually swimming, his head above the waves as his limbs carried him, fighting the powerful drag of the current. Faces moved, following his progress. His father's was not one of them.

Jeremy's hands were shaking. He couldn't tell if he was breathing. He had always wondered what this moment would be like, if he was ever brave enough to meet it.

What if, in the in-between, you had a chance to be yourself?

He reached Evan's side. His father broke off shouting mid-word, the last person in the restaurant to notice his son. His mouth was open, his eyes bloodshot, his cheeks splotched with red.

Jeremy looked directly into his father's face.

He reached out.

He took Evan's hand.

Evan stiffened, then let out a soft "Hah!" and squeezed Jeremy's fingers tight. Jeremy squeezed back, stepping in close so their shoulders touched.

They stood there, two boys holding hands, being looked at by every single person in the restaurant.

Time shimmered to a stop.

Jeremy kept his eyes fixed on his father. He was staring, like everyone else, but Jeremy could tell that beyond that he was also finally seeing. There could be no mistaking what the boys' closeness meant, and Jeremy watched understanding ripple through his father's drenched, swaying brain. He saw the bloodshot eyes widen in shock, then harden, then fold down into slits under pressing brows.

Jeremy gripped Evan's hand, bracing.

"I don't—" his father said. His mouth closed, then opened. "So you—"

But he never finished. One of the other diners coughed, and at the sound Jeremy's father's awareness shifted, expanding to encompass not only Jeremy and Evan but the whole silent, attentive room. He jerked around, startled, taking in the booths and tables full of people. Reading their expressions.

Jeremy saw the exact moment shame came into his father's eyes.

He stood alone, exposed, the drunken center of clear-eyed public judgment. His shoulders hunched as the last glow of anger visibly died, replaced by a sharp, cringing embarrassment. In one movement, he staggered forward, collapsed onto an abandoned chair, and dropped his head to the table.

Like the lights coming on at a theater, the crowd filling Sandy's Grill started to talk.

Looking back on that night, Jeremy always remembered what came next in a series of flashes: the man from the next booth helping Sandy get his father out to the parking lot. His father, floppy-armed and mumbling, being hauled into the back of Sandy's car. Sandy behind the wheel, Evan riding beside her. The weight of his father's body as Jeremy struggled to keep him upright on the curves.

He remembered the sound of his father collapsing onto the

groaning springs of his bed. Sandy squeezing his shoulders before she sped back to her restaurant full of scandalized customers. The burning moment hand in hand with Evan on the porch, when what he'd just done—what they'd both just done—could matter and echo between them like it should.

He remembered Evan's fierce, endless hug good night. The click as the door swung closed. The brief hum of silence in the beach house, then the hollow rumble of his father's low, juddering snores.

Thirty-One

MONDAY, JULY 9

A little after nine the next morning, Jeremy, in a clean T-shirt and jeans, his hair still wet from the shower and his borders and boundaries down for the first time in his life, stepped out onto the porch of the beach house.

He went to the railing and perched in his usual spot, squinting at a scattering of kites dancing their colors against the overcast sky. The wind searched his drying bangs. He did not look over at his dad in the rocking chair.

His dad was wrapped in the quilt from the downstairs bedroom. His face was gray, his forehead wrinkled over his aviator sunglasses, pressing down as though trying to crush or bury something. Salt-and-pepper stubble ran across his cheeks. An untouched mug of coffee sat on the deck beside him.

"Jeremy," he said.

"Dad."

The silence resumed, leaving room for the echo of shouted words, slurred anger, and shaking defiance from the night before. Plenty of things had been revealed at the Grill. Plenty of things had been brought out into the open, publicly and permanently. By both of them.

Jeremy had thought it over as he lay staring up into the darkness through the long, long night. He had come out. He had done it. He had stood up in front of his father and everyone and claimed what he felt for Evan. Claimed the right to know his own heart. And he could never take it back.

He was proud, in the most basic sense, of what he had done. Shaken, sure, and still more than a little scared, but proud.

That couldn't be the case for his dad, though, who had been outed, too, in a way. Jeremy would have that memory of him, and all it meant, burned into his mind from now on. His father had fallen hard at the exact moment Jeremy was stepping up.

Jeremy had already surprised himself that morning by deciding to join his dad on the porch. He did it again by being the one to break the silence.

"What's it like?" he asked, finally looking over.

"What's what like?"

"A hangover."

His father's eyebrows appeared over his sunglasses, his gaze still fixed on the flat white sky and the water stretching to the horizon.

"It's like a room," his father said at last. "A small room. Cramped, and dark, and . . . clammy, like in a basement. And you can't get out for hours and hours. Sometimes whole days. And every time you wake up there, you swear it'll be the last time, because you hate it. Like, if anyone ever held the door open and said, *Want to go spend part of your life in there?* you'd say heck no. But you do go. Over and over and over, you go back in. Until waking up in there starts to feel familiar, then normal. Then like your home."

Jeremy sat on his railing, trying to imagine the things his father was telling him. Trying to understand why anyone would think being drunk and then hungover was better than the alternative. Trying to push away the uncomfortable prickle of recognition at the idea of a personal prison you couldn't stop seeking some sort of refuge in.

"I'm pretty ashamed of what you saw yesterday, Jer. Obviously." His father's voice was scratchy. "I'm ashamed of what I said and what I did, and how everyone saw, and that I put you in the position of having to be the parent and try and stop me. It was wrong. I was wrong."

He sat up, leaning his head against the brown wall of the house, letting out a long breath. "You reach this point in your life, and you think you've got it all figured out. You've got the wife, the house, the kid, the job. All the pieces; you're a grown-up. And then bang, it falls apart. And where does it go? What are you supposed to do? Everything you did before is exactly what got you here. Nothing that used to work does anymore. Nothing fits. How are you supposed to figure out what to do next?"

His aviators flashed as he tilted his face toward Jeremy.

"Seems like you've got some stuff figured out, though, huh?"

Jeremy had been waiting for it, but he still winced. He gave a half nod, his jaw tight.

"So . . . is this Evan kid your boyfriend?"

Jeremy almost fell off the railing. It was not the question he'd been bracing for. Not at all.

And he had no clue how to answer.

Were he and Evan boyfriends? Was that what holding hands and sneaking out together and making up your own coded language meant? He knew how big his feelings were, but he couldn't say the same about Evan. Not to that level. Not even with *Cassin's auklet*. Was he supposed to just ask? Was one of them supposed to say something? What would being boyfriends even mean anyway, with him leaving tomorrow?

"I don't . . ." Jeremy began. He closed his mouth, opened it. "It's not . . ."

His father gave him a moment, then grunted. "It's okay, I get it. I mostly just wanted you to hear from me that, you know: It's okay."

Silence settled over the porch again.

"Guess we slid right past each other this trip, huh?" Jeremy's dad said after a while, bending down to retrieve his coffee. "You've been busy growing up. I've been . . . doing something else." He took a sip, made a face, wavered over holding the coffee or setting it back down, and in a flare of frustration just flung the mug out over the railing. They heard it shatter.

"Jer. I want you to know that things— I— It won't be like this. Back home. I kinda freaked out a bit. The divorce. Then living out here, trying to be a solo parent. And my brother around. You know how we are. Plus, you're getting older, and that's gonna mean some distance, and I just—I don't want you to think—I'm not always . . ." He blew out his cheeks. "I should shut up until I know what I mean, shouldn't I?"

Jeremy didn't answer. They both sat, sorting things out, while the wind poured in from the water to the land.

"Man," said Jeremy's dad, rubbing his forehead, "have there always been this many birds screaming around here? Can't believe I never noticed."

A laugh escaped Jeremy before he could stop it. "American bittern," he said, half to himself.

"Is that what they are?" asked his dad.

Jeremy coughed and straightened. "No." He looked up at the sky. "These are Heermann's gulls, mostly. The other one is just from a code Evan and I came up with. It means *feeling awful.*"

It was his dad's turn to laugh. "You got that right." He pulled off his sunglasses and squinted out along the beach. "Heermann's gulls. You told me that our first day. I remember."

Over on the railing, Jeremy swallowed. Something else had occurred to him in his long night's thinking, something he needed to do, and the urge to get it over and done with rose in him. "Hey, Dad?" he said. "I'm, uh, I'm sorry, too. For not noticing, on this trip. Stuff you did for me. You know, like the sparklers, and the lasagna, and . . . stuff." There was more, but in that moment, it was as much as he could manage.

His dad looked over, still squinting. "Hey," he rumbled. "You're my boy. I love you."

With that, Jeremy decided he and his father had shared enough for one morning.

He got up, limping on a foot that had fallen asleep, running a hand through his hair to avoid the possibility of eye contact. "Okay, I'm, uh, gonna get breakfast and then start packing."

"Right." His dad nodded, then winced. "I'll start soon, too. I just—need a bit more time."

"Do you, you know, need anything?" Jeremy had no idea what his dad might need, but his mom would expect him to ask.

"Nah, Becker'll be around soon. I guess Sandy called him to come back early. He'll fix me up. You shouldn't have to deal with this, Jer. Thanks." There was an edge to his father's voice. Jeremy couldn't tell if it was anger at himself or at the idea of being nursed through a hangover by his younger brother. He guessed it was probably both.

Jeremy went inside, made toast and cereal, and took everything upstairs. He checked his phone, but there hadn't been any texts from Evan since they'd agreed to meet outside the store at eleven.

He ate, then pulled out his bags and surveyed the room. He didn't really want to pack, no matter what he'd told his dad out on the porch. Packing meant leaving. Packing meant goodbye. But tomorrow there would be cleaning to do, so packing now would mean the maximum amount of time with Evan for the rest of this final day.

Reluctantly, he got started.

Coming downstairs an hour later, Jeremy heard the shower running and found his uncle fussing over one of the cabinet doors in the kitchen.

"Never used to wobble like this," Becker said as Jeremy came in. "Your dad's getting cleaned up, little man." He set down his screwdriver, crossed the kitchen in four strides, and wrapped Jeremy in a sudden, enveloping hug. Jeremy stiffened, then hugged him back awkwardly. It was the first time he could remember his uncle hugging him since he was small. It went on a surprisingly long time, like Becker was trying to convince him of something, and Jeremy felt himself relax just the tiniest bit.

With one final squeeze, Becker let him go and returned to the wobbly cupboard. Jeremy, blinking, headed for the fridge.

"So, I hear you like guys," Becker said.

Jeremy's shoes caught on the linoleum. He grabbed for the counter, narrowly missing the bubbling coffeepot, and heard himself gasp out, "Yeah, so far."

Becker grinned at him around the cabinet. "Right on. Anyway, I've got some things to fix up before the next renters come to stay. You okay if I'm around?"

Jeremy managed to nod. "Sure. I'm heading into town anyway."

"Cool. And mind if I turn on the radio? Really loud classic rock is a guaranteed cure for a wicked hangover. Your dad will thank me."

Screaming vocals and wailing guitars followed Jeremy as he headed out the door and down the steps. But it was his uncle's *Right on* that rang in his ears.

That was it? That was all Becker had to say? Jeremy had prepared himself for teasing, bad jokes, disappointment even. Not a grin and a *Right on.* He was actually shocked. His dad's and uncle's reactions had been the ones worrying him most as he'd stared up at his ceiling through the night. Now both of them were over and done with, and somehow, he was still fine.

Smiling his first full smile of the morning, Jeremy headed up the gravel driveway toward Rosemont and into his last full day on the coast.

Thirty-Two

"So, did your grandma hear about last night?" Jeremy asked Evan, flicking a piece of gravel across the grass.

They were back in their spot at Lookout Park. The overcast day had gotten hot, and the wind was cooler up here than in town. Evan sat cross-legged beside him in shorts and a faded yellow tank top. A pack of teenagers was blasting music at one of the nearby picnic tables, occasionally screaming with laughter. To their right, two women in their thirties were wrangling toddlers onto a patch of blankets. Something had gone wrong with an applesauce squeezy and one of the toddlers was crying.

"Yeah. I filled her in on everything before I left."

"Everything?"

"Everything."

"And . . . how'd it go?"

Evan picked up his own handful of gravel and threw it. "It went okay. She wasn't happy to hear about what happened with your dad. But she likes you a lot, so, you know." He tilted his head, watching a group of spotted sandpipers riding an updraft above them. "How 'bout you? You talk to your dad?"

Jeremy nodded. "My uncle, too, actually. He's back. I guess my dad told him about us."

"What'd your uncle have to say?"

"Right on."

Evan smiled. "And your dad?"

"He was doing pretty rough this morning but he—he said he was sorry for last night. And he, uh, he asked if we were, you know, um . . . boyfriends."

It was the first time Jeremy had said the word anywhere but inside his own head, and to his well-worn instincts it felt like setting off a firework. He braced himself for the sandpipers to wheel away in shock, and the teenagers' music to screech to a halt, and the toddlers fighting over a spilled Tupperware of grapes to stop and stare.

But the world ignored him and carried on, busy with its own concerns, and Jeremy had the smile curling the corners of Evan's mouth all to himself.

It was a surprised smile, bright and sweet. But it wasn't enough to answer the question now pressing over the day like the high white clouds: *So, are we?*

One of the circling sandpipers called out once, twice, its silver body slashing against the sky as Evan leaned over and pressed his lips to the top of Jeremy's shoulder, right where the seams of his T-shirt met.

Jeremy had not known feelings like the ones he was having were possible. Time, already slowed to honey, stopped. He could feel each individual piece of gravel under his hands. He could feel the weight of Evan all the way to the bottoms of his feet.

Small sparks of panic skittered across the surface of his mind— what if the teenagers caught them? What if the two moms looked over? But to his joy, Jeremy found he was stronger than he had been. The old fears rose up, then blew away. The perfect moment remained, still happening in his real life, on this real day, to him.

Evan's head lifted and time whirred back to normal. Jeremy took a breath. They were two boys sitting side by side, closer now, their knees touching, their faces turned to the horizon.

Jeremy felt like it would have been the easiest thing in the world to take Evan's hand, jump from the park down to the beach in one massive leap, and go running off like giants across the sea, just the two of them.

"I wish . . ." he managed before stopping to clear his throat. "I mean, don't you— Wouldn't it be great if everyone else was gone? Just for today?"

"Like, have the whole town to ourselves?"

"Yeah."

"Oh, totally."

"Totally."

"Only, why just today?" Evan said. "Why not have it for an entire summer? Or forever?" He tapped his knee against Jeremy's. "Say every other person in this town disappeared, right now, and we never had to leave. What would we do?"

"This." Jeremy grinned. "Then go to Sandy's and make massive ice cream sundaes."

"Yeah." Evan was nodding. "And collect all the best gems and fossils and things from Mr. Sharma's shop and use them to make my fort the coolest fort in the entire world."

"And ride shopping carts down the streets playing that old French horn."

"And speak in seabird and nothing else."

"And we could live here forever."

"In our very own town, right here forever."

They decided not to run that afternoon, filling the rest of their day by sharing sodas up and down the streets of Rosemont and hunting shells along the waterline instead. The weather stayed overcast and hot, the clouds only finally breaking up with the beginning of sunset.

Neither of them even considered going home. They answered their texts from Jeremy's dad and Evan's grandmother with short, impatient replies, and somehow the grown-ups seemed to actually understand.

They bought themselves dinner at the gas station mini-mart, loading up on chips and donut snack packs and string cheese and jumbo bottles of iced tea. The driftwood forts were all full for the sunset, so they ate in a hollow between two dunes just off the beach, surrounded by seagrass and clumps of wild lavender. They'd been talking less and less as the day went on, and the silence was almost constant between them as they ate, shielded from the world by the sloping sand, looking down to where the waves met the coast.

The dunes cut most of the onshore wind but not all, and as the last glow faded from the sky and true night fell they cuddled together for warmth, the sand trickling around them as Jeremy curled himself under Evan's shoulder. He could hear Evan's heartbeat though his tank top. Evan began tracing slow shapes and letters across the fabric on Jeremy's back, lifting his hand every now and then to brush through his hair.

They stayed like that for a long time, and Jeremy found his mind wandering in reverse along the emotional mountain range of the last two weeks. The fear and clamor of the diner; the dinosaurs; the cliffs; the unexpected joy in running; the shelves of Tidepool Knickknacks. The swooping punch he'd felt at his very first sight of Evan.

That last thought made him smile, and he closed his eyes, pulling his mind back to the present and the sound of Evan breathing, hanging on as long as possible.

It was Evan who moved first, as always. "Sorry, getting cold," he murmured into Jeremy's hair, and Jeremy, who'd felt him shiver, nodded against his chest.

They pulled apart and stood, gathering up the remains of their dinner and brushing sand off their legs. Overhead the sky had opened to a field of velvet brushed with stars, a yellow moon a few days short of full rising between them. Jeremy gazed up at it, an ache spreading from his heart to the muscles behind his eyes.

Evan was watching him. "Hey," he said softly. "You know I'll run by in the morning."

"Okay."

Evan held out a hand, and Jeremy slid his own into it. Slowly, they walked back along the beach toward town, the moonlight casting one long shadow behind them on the sand.

Thirty-Three

TUESDAY, JULY 10

The inside of the beach house had been tidied. Clothes, toothbrushes, books, and papers had all been boxed and bagged and hauled out front, leaving the freshly dusted furniture ready for the new renters. The windows were closed; the door had been locked. Jeremy and his father no longer lived there.

His father and uncle were arguing now, comfortably and pointlessly, about the best way to fit the bags in the back of the car. Jeremy was in his spot on the railing, a backpack at his feet. He sat watching the beach, staring out at the sand, turning the last white shell over and over in his hands.

He hadn't texted Evan that morning. Helping with his dad's final packing had provided an early distraction, and then there had been the cleaning—the cabinet doors in the kitchen, the corners of the bathroom tile, the gap behind the sofa. Becker, arriving with donuts to see them off, had said to ease up, he wasn't that picky a landlord. But Jeremy had gone ahead anyway, grateful to keep his hands busy and his mind off what was coming.

Now there was nothing left to do but wait.

I'll run by in the morning. That was what Evan had said.

Jeremy was dimly aware his dad wanted to get on the road. He had no idea how much time had passed since they'd locked the door, but it had been more than a while. Maybe Evan had gotten a late start that morning. Maybe he wouldn't come by for hours. It didn't matter; Jeremy would be there.

Another dozen turns of the shell later, his eyes caught a flash of red up the beach: a boy, running fast, his hair a dark blur in the wind.

Jeremy straightened, slung his bag over one shoulder, and went down the steps to the sand.

He threw the shell aside without looking.

Evan slowed as he drew near, easing to a jog, and then he was there, stamping to a stop, bracing his hands on his hips.

"Hey," he said between breaths.

"Hey," said Jeremy.

"My grandma says—to say bye—for her. And that she—really likes you."

"Tell her bye from me, too. And same."

Evan nodded. He paced side to side, bringing his breathing back to normal.

Jeremy glanced over his shoulder in time to see his dad and Becker look away quickly, busying themselves with the car. His dad said something to his uncle, who nodded.

"Hey, Jer?" his dad called out. "Becker thinks I should, uh, check the oil before we hit the road. You okay if the two of us head into town?"

Embarrassed and grateful, Jeremy nodded.

"We'll meet you at the grocery store lot."

"No rush!" called Becker, climbing into his own truck.

Jeremy and Evan stayed silent until the rumble of tires on gravel faded.

"Hi," Jeremy said.

"Hi." Evan, still moving, would not meet his eyes. He kept half raising his face, then glancing away. Finally, he said, "So I wanted to tell you, you know, thanks."

Jeremy blinked. "For what?"

Evan smiled with one side of his mouth. He waved a hand in a loose circle, palm up, a gesture that might have meant *I don't know*, or *everything*.

"Same," Jeremy said, understanding. "And you have a—a good rest of your summer, okay?"

Evan stopped pacing and stepped forward, right into Jeremy's space. "You're *cormorant*, and I think I love you," he said in a rush.

Jeremy threw back his head and laughed. He couldn't help it. Evan was ahead again, just like always.

"You're *cormorant*, and I think I love you, too," he said.

"Okay, so, why're you laughing?"

"Because, just—" Jeremy's heart was doing loops. He dropped his pack and seized Evan, pressing his face to his friend's dark hair. Evan's arms locked around his shoulders.

Time moved on, the two boys did not.

At last Evan shifted, mumbling, "I brought you something."

They separated, the magnet charge still tugging between them as Evan snapped open the side pocket of his shorts.

"Hey, same." Jeremy knelt to his backpack, pulling out a small package neatly wrapped in a page from a magazine.

"Sorry, I didn't wrap mine," said Evan, holding out a closed fist.

"Lazy."

They swapped, and Jeremy found himself holding the little triceratops from the night in Evan's fort.

"You know what you have to do," Evan said.

Jeremy's throat was tight, but he gave his best dinosaur roar. A Heermann's gull overhead wailed a reply.

"Ha!"

The sound of Evan's huffing laugh made Jeremy's stomach ache. That sound was so Evan. So much a part of him. "Open yours," he said.

Evan did, pulling back the glossy paper to reveal a gray-brown lump of stone. "Wait, is this that geode?" he said. "The one you dropped in my shop the day we met?"

Jeremy nodded.

"You still haven't cracked it."

Jeremy nodded again.

Evan looked down at the rock for a long moment, then back at Jeremy. "I'll keep it safe for you."

Jeremy smiled, but his chest hurt. He'd been keeping the geode as the final act, the parting gift, and now that it was done . . .

"So, what else do you have in that bag?" asked Evan.

It was a flimsy reason to keep talking, but Jeremy, relieved, showed him: his worn-in running shoes, the fashion magazines, the turquoise beach glass, the deer bottle cap, the lump of citrine, the tiny bag of shark teeth, the eagle salt and pepper shakers.

"You could start your own knickknack shop with all that," said Evan. "Kinda surprised you're not taking the bird book, though."

"Oh, I totally am." Jeremy spun his bag to show the book nestled in a side pocket.

"Good. So I can text you random bird names sometimes and you'll be able to figure out what I'm saying?"

"Definitely. And you should text me more than sometimes. If you want."

Evan shoved Jeremy's shoulder with the back of his hand. "Course."

They were coming to it now. They could both feel it. An ending.

"Are you gonna— Do you think you'll come back next year?" Evan asked.

Jeremy looked around at the house, the sand, the thundering blue ocean. He wanted to come back. So much. But he couldn't summon a clear vision of his life ahead to imagine it. He hadn't even decided which city he'd be living in when school started. How could be plan for next summer?

And what would he even be like in a year? Or Evan? He tried to picture them reuniting right here on this same stretch of beach: actual teenagers, taller, older, with another Oregon winter under their belts. Would they pick up where they were leaving off? Would they even want to? Would anything they were feeling now be the same?

Jeremy swallowed, gathering in his thoughts. "I don't know," he managed. "I guess—I guess we'll see." He looked away, and a patch of dark birds floating on the waves caught his eye. An idea came to him, and he pointed. "Hey, what are those over there?"

Evan looked. "Common murre. Why?"

"That won't work; it needs to be a good name. Are there any birds you like?"

"Just, like, a random bird?" Evan thought. "Curlew, I guess?"

Jeremy pulled out the book and found it: a speckled wading bird with a long, downturned bill.

"Curlew. That's perfect."

"For?"

"We need a bird that means *goodbye*."

The word slid into the day like rain against a bedroom window. Evan reached for him again.

Somehow they both knew, between their squeezing arms and ribs, when it was done. They pulled away together, hands sliding over elbows, wrists, pausing at the fingertips. And then they were apart, with the wind blowing free between them.

Evan tucked the geode in the pocket of his shorts, double-checking the snaps. He raised his face. His shining eyes found Jeremy's. "So . . . *curlew*," he said.

Jeremy had been afraid of this moment since he'd opened his eyes that morning. He had imagined this exact ache, the urgent need to pull Evan back to him, to keep the contact, to hang on. But he would have to let go sometime.

"*Curlew*," he whispered.

He felt it, the rip in his chest as Evan turned away.

Evan did not look back. Not once. He shifted foot by foot into a jog, then into a run, and all the birds of summer rose up around him, filling the air, wheeling and crying, the shadows of their wings flickering over the beach.

Jeremy stood, watching, until he reached the end of the first long curve. Between the crash of one foaming wave and the next, Evan was gone.

Slowly, squawking and complaining, the birds returned like falling leaves to the sand.

Jeremy moved then, hefting his bag, shrugging it over his shoulders.

He turned, putting the wide Pacific Ocean at his back, and began the quiet walk into town, into the uncertain future that was coming, into whatever new life lay ahead of him beyond the glass, going over the language of seabirds in his mind.

Glossary

Marbled murrelet = *friends*

Heermann's gull = *annoying*

American bittern = *feeling awful*

Sanderling = *happy*

Caspian tern = *high five*

Great blue heron = *hungry*

Cormorant = *beautiful*

Black-footed albatross = *lonely*

Cassin's auklet = *us*

Curlew = *goodbye*

Other Oregon birds seen or named: Horned grebe; cinnamon teal; wandering tattler; snowy plover; osprey; sparrow; chickadee; killdeer; western gull; black-legged kittiwake; sooty shearwater; ruddy turnstone; fork-tailed storm petrel; spotted sandpiper; common murre.

A Note about the Birds

This book, like a summer on the Oregon coast, is full of birds. I love birds and have done my best to describe the ones in this book as accurately as possible, but careful bird-watching readers may notice I've taken liberties when it comes to timing. To put it simply: Most of the birds Jeremy encounters can be found on an Oregon beach in June, but not all.

Those special guest birds who wouldn't ordinarily be around have been included because I couldn't resist their beautiful names. It's a sad but true fact that some bird names just sound sillier than others, and while I certainly love a good canvasback, lesser scaup, bufflehead, American coot, marbled godwit, red knot, gadwall, northern shoveler, short-billed dowitcher, parasitic jaeger, mew gull, or brant, I wanted the majority of birds named in this book to bring a certain romance to the story rather than giggles.

For anyone interested in learning more about the seabirds of Oregon, flipping through this book again and finding all the places I got things wrong could be a fun—and hopefully rewarding—place to start.

Author's Note

While the details of this story are fiction, many are rooted in my own life. Like Jeremy, I fell in love for the first time at the age of twelve, an experience I remember vividly to this day. I also remember the moment immediately after, when I realized what falling in love with another boy might mean. At the time it scared me, and with no idea what else to do, I pushed the love aside and hid the things my heart was telling me. I would end up hiding them for another twelve years.

For LGBTQIA+ kids, the big feelings that often first arrive during the late-elementary years can come with extra complications. Moments that should be happy become snarled in worry or fear, and it can take a long time to get them untangled. Many kids do what I did, learning early to monitor, hide, and tamp down their emotions. Sadly, that often includes the really good ones—like love.

In *The Language of Seabirds*, I wanted to write a story where the main character gets to celebrate big feelings instead of pushing them away. Fear and uncertainty still show up on the page because those things are part of our world, but in this story they don't win.

I chose to hide when I was twelve because I was scared to do anything else. My hope is this story will provide an alternative, a blueprint for another choice. For any reader who might need one.

Acknowledgments

This book very nearly didn't happen. In the summer of 2018, I was preparing a list of project ideas for my agent, wondering what to do next after the fun I'd had writing the silly, pillow-fort-secret-society world of my first two books. The list I came up with was mostly more of the same: rompy *"what if?"* scenarios with an emphasis on magic and comedy. I wrote multipage descriptions of new worlds for my agent, new secret doors and lost keys, new animal sidekicks, new buried treasures, and new superpowers. And then I paused, debating. A title had been nagging at me, a title and not much more, just an image of the beach on the Oregon coast and one boy, a little sad, watching another running fast along the sand. It wasn't much to go on, and nothing at all like what I usually wrote. I hit save, preparing to send in the document as it was. Then, not entirely sure why, I scrolled to the bottom and typed, *The Language of Seabirds: a sad, gay, first-love summer beach story on the Oregon coast? Maybe.*

To my total shock, my agent called the following day to tell me *Seabirds* absolutely had to be my next project, and after three years of writing, rewriting, re-rewriting, pitching, praying, rewriting again, and finally editing, I cannot believe how close I came to letting this story go. This has been a hugely important book for me—writing it literally changed my heart—and that's why my first and biggest thank-you goes to Brent Taylor, of Triada US Literary Agency. You are the greatest champion and cheerleader I could ever hope for, and your instincts are impeccable. *The Language of Seabirds* would not exist without you. I can never say thank you enough.

Next comes the team at Scholastic who gave this book the perfect nest to call home, starting with the spectacular David Levithan. Thank you for seeing the story under the writing, for showing me how to find it, and for giving me the time and grace to do the work. Every word of this book meant breaking new ground for me, both as a writer and a person, and your support, kindness, and care made that possible.

A sky full of thanks to the extraordinary Teo DuVall for making me cry with the perfect cover, to Christopher Stengel for a design and layout that had me sounding like a Heermann's gull, and to my indescribably brilliant publicist, Alex Kelleher-Nagorski. I don't know how you do what you do, but I know I am beyond lucky to have you on my side. Enormous thanks also to Jeffrey West, Melissa Schirmer, and everyone else at Scholastic who has treated this book so well.

Thanks to my family, in all our different skies.

Thanks always to Amber, Lindsey, Gabrielle, and Maria.

Thanks to all the author friends who reached out and reached back as we navigated the pandemic, especially Kelly Jones, Caroline Carlson, J. Anderson Coats, and Lish McBride.

Thanks to Grant Peel for keeping me functioning with the walks and coffees and movie analysis amid the squirrels of Volunteer Park.

Thanks to Wiliama Sanchez for inspiring me to write about a sweet, beautiful guy living in Oregon. And for the flowers. They were gorgeous. I'm still sorry I got so flustered.

Thanks to Danielle Dreger for having one of the world's best salt and pepper shaker collections.

Thanks to Steven Carter-Bailey for being both a sweetie *and* a biscuit.

Thanks to John Paul Brammer, whose book helped me sort out just why fashion was so important to Jeremy (and me, back when I was a queer twelve-year-old).

Thanks to all my local indies, especially Third Place Books, Queen Anne Book Company, University Book Store, and Phinney Books, home of my champion Tom Nissley.

Thanks to Ursula K. Le Guin for every word you ever wrote. *Searoad* had an enormous influence on this book, and I hope you don't mind me giving Jeremy a brief glimpse of Klatsand in tribute.

I believe in celebrating my influences, so readers may also notice tiny nods laced throughout this book to: *Reading Rainbow*; *The Devil Wears Prada* (the movie); *Natasha, Pierre & the Great Comet of 1812* (the musical); Kate Bush's album *Aerial*; Judy Collins's song "Albatross"; *The Secret of Roan Inish* (my favorite movie of all time); Susan Cooper's *The Dark Is Rising*; Elton John's song "The One"; and *A Room with a View* (the movie).

And, last as always, thanks to Alex Kahler. You encouraged me into this gig, the job of my dreams as well as my heart. Thank you for that, and for the bakery visits, the coffees, the long, long talks, and the everything. People reading this probably think we're a couple, but you're my best friend and that's even better.

Okay, I'm cheating, one more:

Thanks to you, dear reader. You are the seabird on the wind. You are the dream and the reason.

WILL TAYLOR is a reader, writer, and honeybee fan. He lives in the heart of downtown Seattle surrounded by all the seagulls and not quite too many teacups. When not writing, he can be found searching for the perfect bakery, talking to trees in parks, and completely losing his cool when he meets longhaired dachshunds. His previous books include *Catch that Dog!*, *Maggie & Abby's Neverending Pillow Fort*, and *Maggie & Abby and the Shipwreck Treehouse*. You can visit him online at willtaylorbooks.com.